Picklewitch stood up and wagged her finger at him. 'The problem with you, Jack, is that you worry too much. This'll be fun. I bet **my** cousin will be the best sort of cousin, you'll see. It's just a fact – like rain and sun and evil cat fudgenuttery.'

But Jack was not at all reassured. If one witch was trouble, then two would definitely be double.

Praise for

PickLewitch & Jack

'A **chuckle-filled** story.'
BookTrust

'Couldn't put it down . . . **100% must read**.'
Ame, age 10, Toppsta

'Everything about this book is **a joy!**'
Book Lover Jo

'Absolutely **whizz-cracking!**'
The Reader Teacher

'A **great** book to share at bedtime.'
Jemt, age 8, Toppsta

'A joy to read aloud.'
Andy Shepherd,
author of *The Boy Who Grew Dragons*

'It's absolutely great. **Very funny.**'
The Teaching Booth

'Absolutely loved this story. **5* from us**.'
Amie, age 9, Toppsta

'Full of heart and giggles.'
My Book Corner

'A joy to read.'
Leon James, age 11, Toppsta

'Love this book . . . full of **fun and mayhem**.'
Poppy, age 6, Toppsta

'Funny and quirky.'
Books for Keeps

'Very **entertaining** indeed.'
Alligator's Mouth

'A **JOY** of a book. Loved every page,
gobbled it up in one afternoon.'
Michelle Harrison, author of *A Pinch of Magic*

About the Author

Claire Barker spent much of her childhood staring out to sea. She has lived in cities, on bright narrowboats and on a little wild farm on the edge of a wood. Once employed to brush Persian cats' fur in a spooky hilltop mansion, she now writes stories in an iron-wheeled hut in Devon. Claire is the author of the Knitbone Pepper series as well as *Picklewitch and Jack*.

About the Illustrator

Teemu Juhani is a Finnish illustrator, comic artist and graphic designer. Born and raised in a land of snow and northern lights, he grew up holding his pencil and dreaming of superheroes. Teemu has studied graphic design and illustration in both Finland and the Netherlands. Currently he's most likely eating some cookies.

CLAIRE BARKER

Picklewitch & Jack
AND THE
CUCKOO COUSIN

Illustrated by
Teemu Juhani

90 YEARS OF EXCELLENCE

FABER & FABER

First published in 2019
by Faber & Faber Limited
Bloomsbury House
74–77 Great Russell Street
London, WC1B 3DA

Typeset by Faber
Printed by CPI Group (UK) Ltd, Croydon CR0 4YY
All rights reserved
Text © Claire Barker, 2019
Illustrations © Teemu Juhani, 2019

A CIP record for this book is available
from the British Library

ISBN 978–0–571–33520–6

FSC
www.fsc.org
MIX
Paper from
responsible sources
FSC® C020471

2 4 6 8 10 9 7 5 3 1

For Julien, who gives me all the best ideas.

1
The Letter

Picklewitch galloped home from school, holding on to her hat and singing at the top of her lungs:

'*NOBODY*
tells ME what to do BECUZ ...
I DUZ what I LIKES
and I LIKES what I DUZ
OH YES!'

Jack ran to keep up, being careful not to step on the cracks in the pavement. 'All I'm trying to say,' he puffed as they reached the driveway, 'is that some cats are quite nice.'

Picklewitch stuck her nose in the air in disgust. 'Well your neighbour's cat PONGS of evil fudgenuttery. I don't knows how you can stand it, it fair makes my eyes water.' She sneezed, as if to emphasise the point. 'Someone should call the police.'

Jack thought about old Fluffchops, about how he slurped milk gummily from a saucer and slept all day. He was about as evil as a bed sock and Jack was going to say as much when Picklewitch kicked the rickety garden gate open.

'Hello, birds! I'm home!' she cried. 'Did you miss me?'

Robins, starlings, crows and sparrows

exploded out of the brambles. They twittered and tweeted, hearts and wings whirring in bliss.

'All right all right, that's enough,' she giggled, batting them away. 'Don't make a fuss, I've only been gone since breakfast! I always come back, don't I? You know you can rely on ol' Picklewitch.'

Jack grinned. His best friend had a missing tooth, bird-nest hair, not to mention a deeply concerning spider pocket. She was grubby, strange, rude, stubborn, gave off a powerful mushroomy whiff and was very, *very* naughty. Despite all this he couldn't help liking her more than anyone he'd ever met.

Jack shut the gate behind them with a click. Before Jack and his mum had moved in, Rookery

Heights had lain empty for years, its large, rambling garden wild and overgrown. Every day strangers had walked by on their way to work, past the boarded-up windows, past its creaking iron gate. No one had any inkling that a little witch was living behind its high garden walls, making magic and playing with the birds.

Sometimes Picklewitch watched the Boxies from the high branches of her walnut tree. If these house-dwellers had looked up from their phones and newspapers they might have caught a glimpse of a lone figure in a pointed hat peering down at them through her cracked binoculars. But people were often too busy to notice the really important things, so her existence stayed as secret as a nut in its shell.

But one wild and windy Thursday, everything changed forever. Quite unexpectedly a big yellow

removal van crunched up the Rookery Heights driveway and a tidy boy got out. Picklewitch took one look at him and decided that she'd had enough of being on her own. It was time to spread her wings and Jack was exactly what she needed – a friend with cake. And when Picklewitch made up her mind there was no simply unmaking it, whether Jack liked it or not.

Even now, watching her conjure up fistfuls of cake crumbs out of thin air, her magic lightning bright, Jack had to pinch himself. How could it be that he lived with a real, twenty-first-century witch? It didn't make any sense, especially to such a logical, sensible boy. But there was no denying that here she was, right in front of his eyes. Picklewitch was as real as rhubarb.

But perhaps the strangest fact of all for Jack was that Picklewitch had chosen *him* as her best friend – a boy who sat alone in the playground every lunchtime – when she could have picked someone popular. He felt very lucky to be her friend, most of the time anyway.

As the last of the crumbs were polished off, a magpie landed on the brim of Picklewitch's hat and carefully tucked a black and white feather into the band. 'Most kind, mister,' she said. 'Proper dandy. Now, last one to the tree's a mugswoggler!' As they hopped over the nettles and brambles, Picklewitch sniffed at the breeze. 'Spring's on its way,' she said, 'mark my words.' Gangs of bluebells jostled with each other and puddles of jelly frog-spawn jiggled with life.

'Badger's pants,' she tutted. 'There's so

much work to do at this time of year. The list in my Grim is already longer than an elephant's nose but I keep remembering extra things.' She pulled a grubby exercise book out of her rucksack. Covered in stickers and stains it said 'PRYVIT' on the front. She flipped it open to a page of chaotic scribbles, took out a stubby pencil and added:

	No. 104 wayke up layzee hedgehogs
	No. 105 Keep burd eggs hot in pokit
	No. 106 sharpen beez stingz

Jack peered over her shoulder. 'Your grimoire's a bit like the journal I keep next to my bed, isn't it? I keep lists in mine too.'

Picklewitch slammed the book shut and shoved it back in her bag, zipping it up tightly. 'How dares you say such a thing?' she hissed. 'Grim has *feelings*.

You know perfectly well he's full of megatronic spells and extra-special witch notes. The same as your book? Ha. A pebble a can never be a peacock, Jack Door.'

Picklewitch often said quite rude things so Jack simply pretended he hadn't heard. He changed the subject instead. 'You haven't forgotten about the lunchtime Nature Club, have you?' he asked as they reached the bottom of her tree. *'Dancing Ant Day?* At school tomorrow? You made lots of big promises and now everyone's looking forward to it.'

Ever since that fateful day when Picklewitch had invited herself into his classroom, life at St Immaculate's School for the Gifted had changed for the better. As Nature followed her to school like an obedient pet, bright green ferns unfurled in inkwells and strands of ivy crept through the keyholes, leaves swirled in the corridors and snails slipped quietly along the bookshelves, patiently munching their way from A to Z. Although the school still had high standards and codes of behaviour, the children had learned to relax and smile a little more, loosening both the knots in their ties and the grip on their textbooks. Even Headmistress Silk was known to sport a wildflower in her suit-lapel these days, although, if asked, she was never able to explain why. Picklewitch's special brand of naughtiness raced down the corridors like the east wind, blowing the dust from the darkest corners. Picklewitch was rule-breaker and a merry maker and with her around the school days sparkled like dewdrops on a cobweb. It came as no surprise to Jack that the other children queued up to join her Nature Club.

'Of course I haven't forgotted,' said Picklewitch,

rubbing her rumbling tummy, 'but I can't do it when I'm hungry. Firstly, I need a cake. Secondly, it must be a massive yumcious galumpher.'

Jack didn't need telling twice. Luckily his mum loved to bake so there were always plenty to go round, much to Picklewitch's delight. Picklewitch *loved* cake. Sometimes at night Jack could even hear her singing about them in her dreams.

'Ohh LADYMUUUM ... *snore*
Cook me a cake
Boil me a BUN *snore*
Fry me a flapjack
Or ... roast me a crumb ...'

Jack turned to go back into the house but was stopped in his tracks by a loud squeal.

'OOO STOP! LOOK, Jack! Up there: a letter!'

Picklewitch gasped, peering through her cracked binoculars.

'For *me*!'

Jack looked up to see a seagull soaring into the garden, a crisp, white envelope clamped firmly in his beak.

'Do witches get letters?' asked Jack, squinting into the sun.

'All the time,' she said.

'Have you ever had one before?'

'No.'

The gull crash-landed at Picklewitch's feet. He blinked a wicked eye and spat out the letter, flapped back up into the air and disappeared over the horizon.

Picklewitch and Jack stared in silence at the envelope lying on the ground.

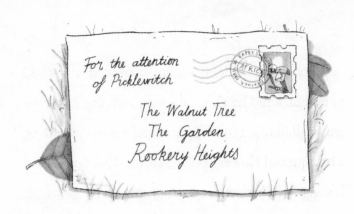

For the attention
of Picklewitch

The Walnut Tree
The Garden
Rookery Heights

The postmark said AFRICA. Jack looked up and scanned the cloudless sky with a frown. Nobody but him knew that a witch lived in his garden. It wasn't the sort of garden you sunbathed in, or mowed, or invited visitors for tea on the lawn. People didn't just *pop by*. The Rookery garden was old and wild and strange, nettles and spiky brambles sprang out from its borders and raggedy black birds patrolled the skies. When the light slanted through in the right way, even the broken brick pathways looked like teeth. Picklewitch's address was supposed to be top secret, as indeed was her magic.

But right now Picklewitch was much too excited to be bothered by that. She tore into the envelope and pulled out a notecard. It had a bunny holding a bouquet of flowers on the front. 'Ooh and look! It's signed *Archie Cuckoo,*' Picklewitch grinned. 'He's coming to stay!'

'Archie Cuckoo? Who's he?'

'Well, I would have thought that was perfectly obvious. He's my cousin, of course.' Picklewitch looked at Jack as if he was the stupidest boy in the world. 'See?' She held it up for him to see. Inside, in swirly ink it did indeed say:

Dearest Picklewitch,

 I am coming to visit.

 I shall arrive at teatime on Tuesday.

from your dear cousin

Archie Cuckoo

'But …' Jack spluttered, 'I thought it was just you and the birds. Why didn't you say you had a family?'

She clambered up into the tree. 'You don't need to know everything,' she said, tapping the side of her nose. 'Witches is mysterious. It's the point.'

'Well …' huffed Jack, feeling rather put out by the unexpected news, 'if you're so *mysterious* then how does this cousin of yours know where you live? I thought *that* was supposed to be a secret too.'

'Maybe the wind told him,' she called down. 'Everyone knows the wind's a blabbermouth.' She dangled from a branch, her legs snipping back and forth like stripy scissors. She looked down at the shadows on the sundial. 'Fudgenuts. Time is getting on and everything must be perfect for when Archie arrives.'

Things were moving much too fast for Jack's

liking. 'Hang on, I didn't think you cared what people thought,' he protested. 'What happened to *"I does what I likes and I likes what I does?"* This sounds very strange to me. What if someone sees? And what about the ants for Nature Club?'

Picklewitch busied about. 'Oh Jack, do be sensible. There's leaves to buff and moss to fluff before I can *even think* about teaching a bunch of ants how to dance.' She stood up, took a tape measure out of her dungarees pocket and measured a raven from beak to claw. 'Oh-dear-oh-no. Most terrible. This won't do at all.' She gave a big sigh and began picking the birds up and moving them about like cans of beans. 'They are all in the wrong order for a start.'

'I *said*,' repeated Jack in a louder voice, determined to make her listen, 'don't you think a pair of witches parading about will be too risky?'

Picklewitch stopped rearranging the birds and glared at him, narrowing her eyes. 'WOT ...' she said, speaking slowly and deliberately, 'do you *mean?*'

Jack's heart beat a little faster. He always felt nervous when she used this particular voice, somewhere between a policeman and a goose. But it *was* true that two witches might attract the wrong sort of attention and if there was one thing Jack dreaded, it was being noticed for the wrong reasons. He knew from his history books that witches got the blame for everything from rainy days to stale bread. Naturally cautious, he was always worried that someone else would figure out their secret: that Picklewitch wasn't just 'theatrical' and that she was in fact a real, live witch. Grown-ups never handled this sort of information well.

'I'm just saying that some people are more

noticeable than others, aren't they?' he coaxed, trying not to stare at her pointed hat and twig-filled hair. One witch was bad but two would stop traffic. 'What am I supposed to tell my mum? What if people start asking questions? What if it's not safe?'

Picklewitch stood up and wagged her finger at him. 'The problem with you, Jack, is that you worry too much. This'll be fun. I bet *my* cousin will be the best sort of cousin, you'll see. It's just a fact – like rain and sun and evil cat fudgenuttery.'

But Jack was not at all reassured. If one witch was trouble, then two would definitely be double.

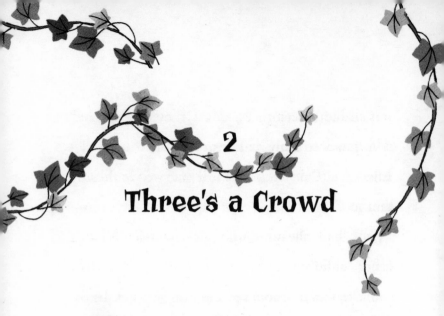

2

Three's a Crowd

Jack woke up bright and early in his little attic bedroom. Keen to get to school, he jumped out of bed and parted his curtains. Down in the garden he could see Picklewitch, already up and hanging a sign in her tree.

WelKum CuZZin
To My Splendiferus Home

His shoulders slumped as he remembered the events of the day before. Jack told himself that it was all about keeping Picklewitch's secret safe, but if he had been truly honest with himself, he would have admitted that something else was bothering him too.

Jack had always found making friends with other children tricky – much trickier than complicated equations or tests. He'd waited ages and ages to find a best friend before Picklewitch came along and now some other witch was coming to stay. They would get on like a house on fire – possibly even SET a house on fire – and he'd be left out again. This made him feel sad, but for some reason the words wouldn't come out in the right way. Instead he just said things that made him sound grumpy.

Jack tried to imagine what Archie would be like as he brushed his teeth (two minutes and forty-three seconds precisely). *I bet he wears a raggedy old cloak. Probably waves a wand about and uses made-up words, just like her. I wouldn't be at all surprised if he has a family of earwigs living in his hair – I bet she'll love that.*

Then another thought occurred to him: *what if Picklewitch wanted to bring this cousin to school?* Oh no. Jack scrubbed his teeth even harder. How would he explain *that* to Victoria Steele. Cake-baker-extraordinaire, bossiest girl in the class and sworn enemy of Picklewitch, Victoria was always looking for a way to get them into trouble.

Jack smoothed his hair down until it shone. Looking presentable was very important at St Immaculate's. The idea of sitting between the two of them in class – the neat filling in a messy sandwich – made his heart sink. Wishing fervently that he'd never heard of Archie Cuckoo, Jack buttoned up his smart blazer, put on his rucksack and trekked out to see Picklewitch.

As soon as he entered the garden Jack could see that the birds were trying super-hard. Normally they were littered all over the tree but today they were lined up, as neat as beads on an abacus. He noticed that some of the cheekier sparrows had bows tied around their beaks to keep them quiet.

Picklewitch was striding up and down a big branch, inspecting the birds and barking orders. She had decorated her hat with postage stamps and feathers and had applied puddle water to press her wild hair down flat. It hadn't worked. In fact, it just made it worse.

'You look ridiculous,' said Jack, a hard knot forming in his tummy. 'Why are you trying so hard?'

'I do not expect a mere Boxie like *you* to understand,' said Picklewitch primly, booting a squirrel into a nearby bush. 'Firstly, he is family and everyone knows that blood is thicker than custard. Secondly, it's tradition: witches must show off to other witches. It is important to have the most beautifulest home.'

'*Beautifulest* isn't even a real word and, while I'm at it, why are you speaking in that stupid voice?' asked Jack, kicking at a stone. 'I don't see what's so special about this witch-boy anyway. He'd better be worth all this fuss. In fact, I bet he doesn't even turn up.'

'Hell-oo!' The garden gate creaked and a voice rang out across the bluebells. 'Coo-ee! Is anyone in?'

3

Two in the Bush

Picklewitch clutched at the front of her dungarees, her eyes as shiny and round as buttons. 'It's HIM,' she gasped. 'He's HERE!' All of Jack's bravado seeped away, as shyness overcame him and he shrank behind the tree.

There, at the garden gate, was a boy. As he walked towards Picklewitch, the bushes and shrubs obediently parted, clearing a path in the undergrowth. Little daisies and violets sprang up wherever he placed his feet.

'Felicitations, dearest cousin Picklewitch,' he waved.

'Salutations, Archie Cuckoo,' piped up Picklewitch, waving back and leaping out of the tree.

For a moment, Jack thought they looked as if they were poised to dance or duel. But as they approached each other, their movements became very peculiar, as stiff and jerky as marionettes. They both bowed and touched noses very gently, reached up into the air and pressed their outstretched fingers together.

> 'Blessed be the sky and air
> Blessed be the bees
> Blessed be the birds and earth
> And blessed be the trees.
> Blessed be the fire and rain

Blessed be us both
Blessed be the witches' code
This shall be our oath.'

'Oh my!' cried Archie, breaking away and twirling around in wonder, his shiny eyes roaming over the leafy canopy. 'It really is a magnificent home! So mighty, even better than I had heard, and your birds are very well-ordered and quiet. Such large, comfortable-looking branches. If you don't mind me saying so, Cousin Picklewitch, this is a truly remarkable example of a *Juglans regia*.'

Picklewitch puffed up like a giant piece of popcorn and grinned. 'I do *not* mind you saying so please-thank-you Archie Cuckoo. I don't like to boast but my tree is the best tree in the garden, in the whole of the street and in the world. In fact, it's the best walnut tree in the universe now I come to think of it.' She turned around. 'Tell him, Jack.'

'Jack?' Archie looked around with a smile. 'Who is Jack?'

'*This* silly fopdoodle,' said Picklewitch affectionately, yanking him out from behind the tree, 'is my best friend, Jack. Say hello to cousin Archie, Jack.'

Jack was lost for words, primarily because Archie was *not at all* what he had been expecting. For a start, he wasn't wearing a raggedy cloak or carrying a wand, nor was there an earwig to be seen. He wasn't even wearing a pointed hat.

In fact, Archie was the opposite of everything Jack had imagined. Dressed in an immaculate grey tailcoat with a silk, horizontal-striped waistcoat beneath, this boy was a picture of order, not chaos. In his gloved hand he held a smart leather briefcase with silver clasps and a combination lock. A gold

watch chain dangled from his pocket and not a hair on his head was out of place. Archie Cuckoo couldn't have looked less like a witch.

Archie cocked his head to one side and then the other, inspecting Jack closely with his bright, golden eyes. He then looked up at the house and a smile spread across his face. '*Ah*, yes, I see. Jack is not like us is he? He's . . .' Jack could see Archie was about to say 'a Boxie', but instead he reached into his waistcoat pocket and handed over his calling card. It was black, embossed with bright silver letters. Jack noticed his grey gloves were very soft, the wrists trimmed with mother-of-pearl buttons. 'Pleased to meet you, Jack. Archie Cuckoo at your service. Any friend of my dear cousin Picklewitch's is a friend of mine.'

Jack's admiring eyes swept down to Archie's briefcase. Picklewitch peered at it over his shoulder. 'Woss-in there then, Archie? Cake, is it?' she asked hopefully. 'Coz I likes cake. I likes cake *a lot.*'

'No, no, nothing as exciting as that, I'm afraid. Just old maps of the world, the oceans and the winds, the stars, you know, that sort of thing.' As Picklewitch's face fell, Jack's lit up.

'What sort of old maps?' blurted Jack, finally finding his tongue.

'Oh, only old explorer maps mostly. Given to me by the great-grandson of Charles Darwin actually.'

'Charles Darwin?' Jack gasped, his shyness forgotten. 'Really? THE Charles Darwin? Jack couldn't believe his ears. He thought about his fellow students: Aamir the Greek scholar, Astrid the astrophysicist, Fenella the Shakespeare expert, the Wilson twins with their telepathic

communication skills – the children at St Immaculate's School for the Gifted were used to amazing sights. But Darwin's maps? Who could fail to be impressed by that? 'That's incredible, Archie!' marvelled Jack. 'Everyone at school would go mad over those!'

'School?' Archie turned to Picklewitch, a curious eyebrow raised. 'What is *school*?'

Picklewitch pulled an old cake wrapper out of her pocket and gave it an idle lick. 'It's a place,' she said, 'where I am more popular than pudding. Everybody loves me. Well, *nearly* everybody. Anybody who's not a fudgenut anyway. We go there most days. Sometimes I likes it so much I even stay until home time.'

Jack's earlier fears about bringing Archie to school were quickly forgotten as he recognised a fellow bright spark. 'I know!' cried Jack, his eyes alive. 'Why don't you come with us today? He can, can't he Picklewitch?' It had not gone unnoticed by Jack that Archie had referred to the walnut tree by its proper Latin name – *Juglans regia*.

'Well . . . I certainly wouldn't want to impose . . .' protested Archie, looking at Picklewitch.

'Oh yes, come on,' implored Jack. 'You're clever and smart and polite. You'll fit right in!'

Picklewitch picked at her teeth with a twig. 'Sorry, we're not going to school today, we are having a day off. I'm going to give Archie a guided tour of my beautifulest garden using the official map.' She pulled out the drawing of the garden that had won them first prize in the Nature project competition. 'We'll be starting in this area *here*,' she said, pointing at the map, 'at *Stabby*. Then we shall move on to *Spiky* – which is *here* – and *Squishy* – which is *here*. But we definitely won't be going over *there* ...' she chuckled, pointing at a bush labelled *BEWARE*, 'because that always ends very badly. I would tell you what lives inside it, but I'm not the sort to give a guest the terrors on the first day.'

Jack wasn't going to give up that easily. '*PLEASE* can he come to school, Picklewitch. The garden will still be here when we get home.'

She gave a heavy sigh and rolled her eyes. 'It's too difficultatious, Jack. I'd have to do a new bamboozle spell to get him in.'

But Jack knew that magic was the only way to get Archie into such an exclusive school at short notice. Indeed Picklewitch had used a bamboozle spell herself to enrol at St Immaculate's on her first day. It stopped grown-ups asking things like *Why is she dressed like that? What's wrong with her hair? What is that smell?* and other such tricky questions. Jack whipped an emergency chocolate muffin out of his pocket and held it temptingly under Picklewitch's nose until she gave in. The whole process took less than a second.

'*And*, as I was about to say, that will be no trouble at all,' she said, licking her lips and rubbing her grubby hands together. 'Chop chop. Follow me!'

4

Schooled

'**N**ow, Archie,' said Picklewitch as she huffed and puffed and blew the creaky school gates open. 'There's five things you need to know about *school*.' She held up four dirty fingers and an even dirtier thumb.

'Fact 1) It's full of foolishness. Would you believe they don't even know about Barnacle Whisper, the bear what does live on the moon? Fact 2) There's a Boxie in there

called Professor Bunsen. Jack
says he's a scientist but I'm pretty
sure he's a Dark Wizard.
Fact 3) Watch out for the bossy
   baker girl. Her sponge cake
   tastes spiteful.
Fact 4) You might think they is
   beautiful waterfalls and try to
   wash in them or maybe even take
   a delicious drink, but **<u>PLEASE
   DO NOT</u>**. They are known as
   toilets and please don't not never
   ask me what they are used for.
Fact 5) There is no fact 5.

She hoicked up her dungarees and straightened
her hat. 'Not everyone can be as clever as me, so
don't feel sad if you don't know the answers in

class. You're my cousin so I'll tell you. Remember: it's never cheating when you're a witch.'

Jack cleared his throat. 'Actually, Archie, don't listen to her. At a school like St Immaculate's it definitely IS cheating whether you are a witch or a Boxie. Cheating is cheating and always very bad, especially here.' At this Picklewitch let out a pig-like snort of laughter.

'Archie,' continued Jack, keen to impress, '*I* would be very happy to help you if you have any questions. I won Most Sensible Boy three years running in my last school and hope to become Head of House this year.'

Archie smiled. 'Thank you Jack, that is most kind.' Jack glowed with pride. He was pleased to notice that, so far, Archie hadn't said anything strange. There hadn't been a single potzblitz, lubberwort or dozy-pox, not one mugswoggler, fudgenut or hobbledehoy. Not only this, as Archie's heels clicked smartly along the cobbles, occasional flashes of gold shone from his socks. Even though they were far from the school regulation black ones, Jack couldn't help but be very impressed.

'Just a couple of things, Archie,' said Jack, as they reached the school steps. 'The first is *no bamboozling my mum*. She's completely off limits, ok? The second is a bit difficult, I know. Please don't use magic within the walls of St Immaculate's.' His hand rested on the door. 'The idea is to blend in, you see. I don't mean to be rude but some people don't like the idea of ... you know ...' Jack looked awkward and lowered his voice to a whisper ' ...*witches.*'

Archie tapped the side of his nose and winked. 'Don't worry, Jack, I completely understand. Your secret is safe with me. *Better to be safe than sorry* is my personal motto.'

Archie's motto was the same as his own! Jack held the school door open for his new friend to walk through.

Archie was sensible and smart and clever and Jack liked him more with every passing moment. They had so much in common. If Picklewitch had more relatives like this then they were welcome to come and stay whenever they wanted! He cast a glance at Picklewitch, who was dawdling behind, shaking the sparrows from her hair and muttering an assortment of rude words. *Can they really be related?* he marvelled. *They're as different as night and day.*

When the last sparrow had been ejected, Picklewitch sprang up the steps and followed them both into the classroom.

Professor Bright was standing at the front,

scowling at an equation on the board. 'Here we go,'
said Picklewitch, cracking her knuckles. 'A special
Bamboozle spell coming right up.' She cleared her
throat, hacked and spluttered and eventually, with
a strangled cry of *'moonpuff'*, she coughed up a
single walnut. She spat it into her fist, cracked it in
two and placed both halves into her front pocket.
'All done,' she sniffed, rocking on her boot heels.

Jack watched Professor Bright's expression gradually soften. His frown relaxed, the corners of his mouth turned up and he gave a happy sigh. An observant boy, Jack had noticed that everyone seemed to have a different bamboozle insect. The one time his mother had been bamboozled it was a moth. Professor Bright's was always a fat bumble bee. It flew out of his ear and bobbed and buzzed away down the corridor, taking all doubts and worries with him. Then, his eyes glistening, the teacher reached through the window, plucked a rose and placed it between his teeth. The transformation was complete.

Picklewitch took Archie's hand and marched up to their form tutor. 'Oi. Pay attention, Teacherman,' she said, taking the rose from his mouth. 'This 'ere is my special cousin Archie and he'll be staying with ol' Picklewitch for a bit. If you look in the register you'll see he's already in there so there's nothing to worry your funny flat hat about.'

'Oh, Picklewitch, family is SO important,' nodded the professor. He ran his finger down the list. 'Oh yes! Here it is in black and white: *Mr Archie Cuckoo.* How odd! I don't remember him being there earlier but you know how much I like surprises!'

Archie put down his briefcase, puffed out his chest and held out a gloved hand. 'A pleasure to meet you, sir, and might I say it's an honour to attend such a special institution as St Immaculate's School for the Gifted.'

'Goodness,' said Professor Bright, wincing slightly under the pressure. 'What a firm handshake you have, Archie.'

'Thank you, sir,' said Archie. 'Where would you like me to sit?'

Picklewitch was already dragging a chair across the room, its metal legs scraping the floor. 'Pssst Archie! Over here! Archie! Come and sit by me and Jack!'

Jack sat sandwiched between them; the girl in a witch's hat and the boy in a smart grey suit, feeling as happy as could be. Not long ago Jack hadn't had a single friend but now he had *two*. He couldn't believe his luck. Also, everybody knew that three friends made a gang. Admittedly it was a weird gang, but it was definitely better than *no* gang. He felt very cheerful indeed.

Victoria spotted the new boy and wasted no time in finding out more. She marched up to their desk, lips pursed. 'Who's this person then, Jack? Another mysterious *friend*? Where DO you find them?'

Jack was about to tell her to get lost when Archie stood up and held out his hand. 'Ah Victoria! My

name is Archie Cuckoo. Very pleased to meet you. I hear you bake delicious cakes.'

Victoria blushed but was determined not to be won over that easily. 'I haven't even introduced myself yet and yet *somehow* you know my name. Hmm. Such an unusual outfit too.' She lowered her voice, leaned over the desk and hissed at Jack: '*Is he magic as well? Is that his so-called gift?*'

Shocked into silence, Jack didn't know what to say. Was it that obvious? But he didn't look a bit like a witch. Luckily Archie saved the day with a good-natured chuckle.

'Oh, Victoria, this must be the great sense of humour I've heard so much about.' Jack looked across at Archie and marvelled at the quickness of his lie. His brain was as fast as lightning. 'No,' continued Archie with a smile, 'my special gift is the study of Entomology.'

'Insects?' Jack looked up at Archie, pleasantly surprised. *Was that bit true? Why hadn't Archie mentioned that before?*

'Creepy crawlies?' Victoria looked disgusted. 'Well, you and Professor Bunsen are going to get on. He likes bugs and other awful things. He's a world famous Lepidopterist, you know.'

Picklewitch scowled. She hoicked a big hairy spider out of her pocket and lowered it slowly and deliberately onto the desk, right in front of Victoria, in the hope it would scare her off.

'Yes, I've heard,' said Archie. He looked around at the tall bookshelves and Latin mottos over the doorways, blinking his golden eyes in wonder. 'What an interesting place this is. I think I'm going to like it here. You know it's strange, but I feel completely at home already.'

5

The Voice of Reason

Unfortunately for Picklewitch, Professor Septimus Bunsen was immune to her Bamboozle spell, no matter how hard she tried. This infuriated her. Jack was sure that it was because he was a proper scientist who had never had an illogical thought in his life.

Professor Bunsen scowled at Archie's name in the register. 'Archie Cuckoo? Who is this boy? No one told me there were going to be extra students today.' Professor Bright chose this moment to poke his head around the door. 'Don't worry,

Septimus, he's splendid, a perfectly splendid boy!'
Picklewitch winked at Jack, and did a double
thumbs-up.

Grumpy as ever, Professor Bunsen turned on
the projector and pointed at the screen. 'Who
can tell me what these are? Let's get on with it.
Quickly. Someone?' The slide showed a selection
of caterpillars and Jack was just about to say so,
when Archie raised his hand and spoke. 'Sir, that
is the larval stage of the order Lepidoptera.'

Professor Bunsen looked at Archie, a single
bushy eyebrow raised. 'Yes. That is correct. Go
on,' he said.

'Thank you, sir. It is something of a special
interest of mine. I believe they are examples of
the Nymphalide family, part of the super-family
known as Papilionoidea.'

The whole class turned to stare at Archie

in admiration. Jack noticed that the corners of Professor Bunsen's moustache began to twitch. Was he actually going to smile? Everyone knew he had *never* done that!

'Well, well. Your knowledge is impressive young man,' said Professor Bunsen. 'It is rare I meet a pupil with such expert knowledge of caterpillars.'

Picklewitch looked smug. 'See?' she whispered to Jack. 'I told you my cousin would be the best sort of cousin.' She put her hand up.

Professor Bunsen's eyebrows dropped into a frown. 'Oh. It's you. What is it now?'

'I just wanted to say that caterpillars is very good for making stencils. They can even munch words out of leaves, if you don't mind helping them out with difficult spellings. I always keep a few in my rucksack, just in case I need to leave a rude message when I'm out and about.'

Everyone laughed, except for Jack, Archie and Professor Bunsen. The rest of the class always thought she was joking, but of course she was deadly serious.

Silently, the professor made a black mark next to her name in the register, next to the six earlier ones from the previous day. Then he crossed over to a pair of red velvet curtains and placed his hand around the rope, dangling at the side.

'Children, today I am going to tell you about my ground-breaking new project. As you know, St Immaculate's School for the Gifted is involved in very important pioneering research with Cambridge University. I have personally gathered caterpillars of every butterfly and moth in Europe. My plan is to study them closely and publish my research in my new book, *Creep, Crawl, Fly*.' He looked over at Archie. 'I think *you* in particular, young man, will appreciate this.' The professor turned back to the class. 'It is with great pleasure I reveal to you my special collection.' He tugged the rope and the curtain slid back to reveal an adjacent laboratory, bright with lights. Inside were dozens of cages filled with armies of caterpillars, dutifully eating leaves.

Picklewitch had opinions on cages. These opinions were strong on a good day and violent on a bad one. She knitted her eyebrows together and growled.

'PLEASE don't do any magic, Picklewitch, not here,' whispered Jack, recognising the warning signs and tugging at her sleeve. 'Remember last time, when you brought the dead butterflies to life? There was so much screaming.'

Picklewitch's fists were clenched, knuckles white. 'But THAT is a wriggler prison. They

belong in the wild. It is my duty as a witch to free them *right now.'*

'No, no it isn't,' said Jack, in what he hoped was a soothing voice. 'I'm sure these little caterpillars will be released when the time is exactly right . . .'

'Now cousin Picklewitch, be reasonable,' whispered Archie. 'This is clearly the best place for them. Look at all that delicious greenery; look at how it's making them nice and fat. It's like a luxury buffet in there! What a marvellous opportunity to study the natural world. Face it, it's the only way Boxies can learn what we, as witches, already know. It's very educational for them. It will help them to understand.'

Picklewitch pondered on this for a moment. She rummaged around in her hair until she found a hairy black and orange caterpillar. She held it up to her ear and listened, nodding and tutting. Then she whispered something back and before long the caterpillar was on the desk, busy munching the word FUDGENUT out of a leaf. However, to Jack's amazement, she caused no more trouble for the rest of the lesson.

Jack was delighted. Had she accepted Archie's explanation, just like that? Whenever *he* told her what to do it just seemed to make the situation worse. In fact sometimes he suspected she did things because he specifically told her not to. *Maybe it's because he's a witch and not just a Boxie,* he thought. Whatever the answer, it was a big relief. Having Archie around was turning out to be a blessing in disguise.

6

Antsypants

The lesson ended and the bell rang for lunchtime break. This meant one thing: Nature Club! Picklewitch held her Nature Club behind the PE shed. It was always very well attended, with membership badges and songs. It all went down so well that some of the other children even tried styling their hair like Picklewitch's. She ran classes to show them how to do it but theirs was never dirty enough to get the desired effect. Hers managed to be stiff, sticky, scratchy *and* greasy all at the same time.

To say she was proud of her special texture was an understatement.

Occasionally at Nature Club Picklewitch snuck in some low-grade middling magic, but to keep Jack happy she managed to make it look like nothing more than a trick, like when she made some ladybirds change their spots, or the time she turned a pine cone into an ice-cream cone. But there was *always* a big crowd and she was *always* in the heart of it.

Picklewitch turned to her cousin. 'Now Archie, I listened to what you said this morning, because you know my manners are very good and manners is important to witches.' She took a deep breath in and made herself as tall as she could. 'But now Picklewitch is going to teach you a thing or five about teaching Boxies. Watch and learn.' She cleared her throat and began.

'Today in Nature Club,' she announced to the gathered crowd, 'I will be teaching you many interesting things. Mostly I shall be teaching ants to march in a straight line.' Normally there was a cheer or a round of applause at this point, but today there was just a general dissatisfied mutter.

Angus Pilkington-Storm put up his hand. 'Excuse me, Picklewitch. The other day you promised to show us *dancing* ants.'

'Yes,' said Fenella, 'because don't ants walk in a line anyway?' There was a general nodding in the crowd. 'I'm sure I've seen them doing that very thing on my patio.'

The Wilson twins chorused in stereo, 'Picklewitch – your hat! Are they supposed to be escaping like that?'

Picklewitch grabbed at the ants as they spilled out like punctuation marks. 'What? No ... I

mean yes ... ha ha, that tickles ... Look, I have been VERY busy lately, what with letters and unexpected visitors. Ants walking in a line is absolutely the best I can do for now,' she said in an irritated voice, 'so you'll have to like it or lump it. Either that or we can play Catch the Ant.'

Everybody shuffled their feet and looked sideways at each other. Jack felt uncomfortable; in comparison to her other tricks, ants walking in a line wasn't exactly a showstopper.

'I'm sure she has something else she can show us in a minute,' Jack said as the atmosphere became increasingly tense, 'because she's really good at this sort of thing, aren't you, Picklewitch?'

But Picklewitch was

already in a state of sulk, arms folded, lips pressed together in a thin, disapproving line and refused to say anything more on the subject.

Archie stepped forward. 'If you don't mind, Jack, I have a suggestion.'

'Yes Archie?' said Jack hopefully.

'Lately I have been experimenting with flowers.' Archie took a handful of seeds out of his waistcoat pocket. He whispered over them and then blew them hard across the school playing field. No sooner did they touch the ground than flowers began to spring up, one by one: daisies, cornflowers, poppies, swaying in the breeze like multi-coloured flags.

'WOW!' said Angus.

'WOW!' said Fenella.

'WOW!' said Jack.

'Archie,' said Aamir, casting an admiring

glance down at his smart briefcase. 'That's absolutely incredible!'

'Nothing more than an illusionist's trick, I assure you,' smiled Archie.

Victoria decided to stick her nose in. 'Hey Archie,' she smirked, 'have you ever thought of helping Picklewitch to run the Nature Club? It looks like she could do with a helping hand.'

'HELP?' Picklewitch suddenly found her voice. 'ME? I don't need no *help*!' Outraged, she scooped up her ants, tipped them back into her hat and crammed it on her head. 'Just you wait, next week I'll be bringin' all sorts, like ... squirrels and ... bees and ... most probably a Golden Eagle what can knit and count backwards in Chinese! You see if I don't.'

She stormed off, Jack and Archie following. 'Picklewitch, wait!' called Jack. He turned to Archie. 'I'm sorry about this. She's got a terrible temper.'

'Oh don't worry,' chuckled Archie. 'Witches can be troublesome.'

Suddenly Picklewitch began to dance on the spot; she hopped and jumped and twirled, flinging out her arms and shaking her legs. *Fidgeting fudgenuts* I've got ants in my pants now! This is all your fault.'

'Me?' Jack couldn't believe his ears. 'How is it *my* fault?'

'Because it was YOUR idea to bring *him* to school!' She jabbed a finger at Archie. 'And now everyone thinks he's better than me. You and all your science and stuff – you're a bad influence on a witch, you are. You're making him soft.'

Jack had had enough. 'Picklewitch,' he said firmly. 'You're being unreasonable.'

'Well YOU are a **lickspittle!**' she yelled, wriggling around, shaking ants out of her trouser legs.

'Oh dear, I am sorry,' protested Archie meekly. 'I don't want to come between the two of you. What a shame.'

'Picklewitch, come back!' called Jack. But it was too late. She was already stomping out of the school gates and down the road, a flock of starlings following her like a black cloud.

7

Symphonies & Squabbles

The rest of the school day streaked by. It turned out that, by some amazing coincidence, everything Jack liked Archie liked too. When Jack told him he liked fossils, Archie had loads to say about ammonites and trilobites. When Jack said he liked maths Archie showed him how he could recite his seventy-nine times table while hopping on one leg.

Normally, Jack spent much of his day trying to keep Picklewitch out of hot water but with Archie there were no such worries. They had so much in common and best of all there was no need for magic. Jack felt guilty that Picklewitch had gone off in a huff but he was having such a fun time with Archie that by home-time he'd almost forgotten their lunchtime squabble.

After the bell rang, Jack and Archie walked home together talking about constellations, space exploration and travel. Archie had travelled all over the world and he had lots of amazing stories.

Jack's family was very small; he had no cousins or aunts or uncles. It was one of the reasons Rookery Heights had been left to them by his great-aunt – Jack and his mum were the only ones left in the Door family. This made him feel special but also curious about other people's families. He thought that Picklewitch was very lucky to have such a brilliant relative.

The time whizzed by and much too quickly they found themselves in the Rookery Heights driveway. There, pinned to the rickety garden gate was a poster. It said:

WelKum
to the
KonSert

'A concert?' exclaimed Jack. 'Looks like Picklewitch has cheered up again. That's a relief. I wonder what she's up to? Come on, Archie!' They pushed open the gate and stepped beneath the hanging ivy, into the garden.

Picklewitch was standing at the bottom of her tree next to some seats and a table made out of logs. 'There you are,' she said as they entered the garden, 'right on time. Now, the birds tell me I might have been in a bit of a bad mood earlier.

Mayhaps it was something to do with the moon or a breeze in my right trouser leg. Ahem.'

Jack looked at Archie and smiled. That was the best apology they were going to get.

'*Anyway*, I'm all better now and ready to treat you to a musical extravaganza and magnificent feast, the likes of which you have never known.' She turned to Archie and winked. 'Be assured, Archie Cuckoo, it will be much, much better than school.'

Jack and Archie looked up to see that the branches of her tree were weighed down with every sort of bird imaginable. They were shifting from foot to foot, fluttering their wings, quietly tweeping and trilling, twittering and twootling, sounding like an orchestra tuning up.

'Quickly, quickly,' said Picklewitch, shoving spiky holly leaves into her hair for extra drama, 'take your seats, the concert is about to begin!'

Jack and Archie sat down on the logs and waited.

Picklewitch stood in front of the tree, her hair looking wilder than Mozart's. She picked up a twig, cleared her throat and raised her arms in the air. Then, with a dramatic swish of her arm, the concert began.

Jack imagined it was *supposed* to sound powerful and moving. He had guessed it was *meant* to be soaring and impressive. But instead it sounded like a slow, never-ending train wreck as crows cawed, buzzards shrieked, gulls squawked, sparrows chittered and pheasants screeched. Jack was sure at one point he even heard a cockerel crow. Archie and Jack put their hands over their ears. None of it was in time, or in tune, and it was very, *very* loud. 'PICKLEWITCH, STOP!' bellowed Jack. 'IT'S TOO LOUD! PICKLEWITCH, CAN YOU HEAR ME?'

But Picklewitch couldn't hear anything at all, as she had stuffed her ears tightly with feathers. The concert went on and on *and on* for far too long, frightening the squirrels. Finally, when it did eventually screech to a slow and drawn-out halt, Picklewitch turned to her audience and gave a deep and solemn bow.

'There,' she beamed, unplugging the feathers, her eyes round and bright. 'What did you think of that? Marvelicious, eh? Better than a science lesson, yes? YES? And now I'll bet you're starving after all that excitement. But don't worry, because for my

next party trick I'm going to magic up a whizz-
cracking feast!'

With a hop and a skip she leaped up onto the log
table and began to dance a clickety-clack boot-heel
jig. She clicked her fingers and sang:

'Whistle-wish a jelly bean
Candyfloss and cakey dream
Chocolate milk and strawberry cream
Picklewitch is the party queen!'

There was a bright flash and a loud explosion.
Eventually, when everyone stopped choking and
the smoke cleared, an array of dishes appeared at
her feet.

Picklewitch looked down and stamped her boot in frustration. 'Oh fiddlesticks and fudgenuts!'

Jack reached over and held up a bundle of cobwebs on a dirty stick. 'Is this supposed to be candyfloss?' Then he held up a glass of brown muddy water and gave it a sniff. 'Eurghh. I'm not even going to ask what this is.'

Picklewitch forced a grin, showcasing the black gap where a tooth should be. 'There's lots of delicious snacks here. Have one of these fresh toadstools!' She held up a dripping green fungus, looking a bit doubtful. 'They're probably only a bit poisonous ... and ... and this looks just like rice but guess what? It's maggots! Oh so clever,' she said, clattering the plates in an increasingly desperate manner. 'And ... and what about this?' She held out a mud pie. 'I have magicked the finest cake! Well, all right, mayhaps not *exactly* cake but it's brown and chocolate is *also* brown and this you cannot deny! Plus, as you can see, it is full of delicious nutritious ... um ... worms ... Well, anyway, nettle sandwich anyone? Frog-spawn jelly pot? What are you waiting for? Come on! Tuck in!'

Jack and Archie rubbed their sore ears and stared at the squirming feast for a long, silent minute.

'I know,' said Jack eventually. 'Why don't we all go into my house for tea? I bet my mum's baked something nice. I'm sure she'd like to meet you, Archie.'

Archie brightened with relief. 'Really? Oh yes, that would be very nice, yes please, thank you.'

'Hang on a minute,' said Picklewitch, waving her hand across the table. 'What about all this 'ere deliciousness?'

Jack rose to his feet, suddenly impatient. 'What *about* it?' he demanded. 'We can't eat this. Why don't you just admit the spell went wrong?'

Picklewitch stuck out her bottom lip and crossed her arms. 'For your information, Jack Door, food spells is very difficult. As you know I am very, very good at crumb making, but making bigger bits is harder than it looks. Even the greatest witches have trouble with feasts.' Picklewitch turned to her cousin. 'Archie, tell him.'

Archie said nothing, just coughed politely into his handkerchief.

'Look, my ears hurt and I'm really hungry,' sighed Jack. 'Can we just go and eat some real food now please?' He picked up his school bag and headed for the gate. 'Come on, I've had enough of this. Let's go.'

They trooped out of the garden, Picklewitch stomping behind the two boys in a mighty grump. As they entered the kitchen, the familiar sweet scent of baking filled their nostrils. 'Mum, I'm home!' called Jack. 'I've got friends with me – can they stay for tea?'

His mum called from the study: 'Of course! You know your friends are always welcome. There's a mountain of raspberry tarts on the side. Help yourselves!'

Picklewitch, managing to put her sulk behind her, immediately set about ferreting amongst the jam tarts for the biggest one.

'So,' said Jack, 'how long will you be staying, Archie?'

'Just for tonight. I'll be on my way tomorrow.' Archie managed to fit a whole jam tart into his mouth and swallow it in one gulp. 'Goodness, these really are the most delicious tarts I've ever eaten. Your mother really *is* the best baker.'

73

'Do you have to go so soon? You've only just arrived,' protested Jack. He and Archie were getting on so well. 'Can't you stay just a bit longer?'

'I got a lovely mossy branch ready specially for you, Archie,' spluttered Picklewitch, spraying crumbs everywhere. 'I wiped off the slug slime and everything. Just a smidgen of pigeon poo is left on it, that's all. It's perfect.'

Archie said nothing. A heavy silence hung in the air between them, until Jack finally broke it.

'You can sleep on my bedroom floor in a sleeping bag if you like, Archie,' blurted Jack, 'I've got plenty of room.'

Archie beamed at Jack. 'Oh Jack. Really? That would be perfect, thank you. I was hoping you'd say that. How kind. I sleep *so* much better inside.'

Picklewitch slammed her fist down on the table and made everyone jump. 'NO. NONONO.

Archie Cuckoo is MY cousin and he's come to visit ME in MY beautifulest house and now you, Jack Door, is stealing him from right under my nose holes!' She turned to Archie and jabbed an accusing finger at him. 'And as for you, Archie Cuckoo ... what do you mean by saying you "sleep so much better inside"? What? Like a *Boxie*? What kind of witch says something like that?' She licked her finger and held it up in the air. 'Feel that. Not a wisp of wind in here! Not to mention crinkle-crankle stairs and all kinds of unnecessary fandangling trumpery.'

'Don't be daft, Picklewitch,' said Jack, 'it's only for one night.'

'One night or forty-twelve, it's not the point,' ranted Picklewitch. She flicked Jack on the end of his nose. 'YOU is being a rotten friend,' she said, 'and YOU, Archie Cuckoo, is an ungrateful and sorry excuse for a witch.' She squinted suspiciously at her cousin, at his smart suit and briefcase. 'And while we're on the subject, why's you so tidy? *Why's you good?* I'm thinking it's very peculiar for a witch.'

Steaming cross, she filled her hat brimful of tarts, chucking them in one by one. 'Suits yerself. I'm not staying here to put up with this fudgenuttery. I'm going home to the birds. They appreciate me.' Then she opened the back door and slammed it behind her. After she had gone, everything was very quiet.

'She's right,' sighed Jack, feeling guilty. 'I *am* being a rotten friend. She put a lot of effort into that concert and I didn't even say thank you. So what if her spell didn't work? And she's right, she IS really good at crumbs. I bet she's feeling left out.' He knew all too well how that felt. Jack put

his hand on the door latch and clicked it open. 'I was just tired and hungry and wasn't as kind as I could have been. I'm going to go and find her and say sorry.'

'Jack,' said Archie, leaning heavily on the door and clicking the latch shut again. 'You are being too hard on yourself. You are *such* a good friend. I think you should just let her get a good night's sleep, then she will feel so much better. Might I say I know that if you were *my* best friend then I would do my best to make sure we never fell out. My dear cousin is so lucky to have you. Loyalty is SO important.'

As Jack brushed his teeth later that evening he marvelled at how different two cousins could be. Archie was as polite and reasonable as Picklewitch was rude and difficult. Jack had wanted to speak to Picklewitch but Archie had made him see sense. Sleeping on it *was* the best idea, he could see that now.

Jack's thoughts drifted to Archie's briefcase and the brisk 'click' the two clasps made. It even had a combination lock. He made a mental note to add 'briefcase' to the Christmas list in his journal. It was such a shame Archie couldn't stay because he was exactly the sort of friend he'd hoped to make when he first came to St Immaculate's. Picklewitch was brilliant in so many ways but you would be mad not to see that he and Archie were a great match.

Jack switched off the bathroom light and padded down the corridor to his bedroom. For the first time ever he would have another boy staying for a sleepover! He wondered if it would be like having a brother. Ever since he could remember it had just been him and mum, and they were very close, but sometimes he wondered what it would be like to be part of a bigger family. He hoped Archie wouldn't be too uncomfortable on the wooden floorboards, but at least it would be better than a mossy, pooey tree branch.

Jack looked through the bedroom door and his heart plunged with disappointment. The sleeping bag on the floor was empty! Had Archie left?

But as he turned the corner, he realised that he had got the wrong end of the stick. Jack's eyes scrolled up over the bed and there, sitting up, tucked beneath the covers, gold socks sticking out of the end, was Archie.

'Ah Jack,' said Archie, browsing through one of Jack's books. 'I've decided to sleep in your bed rather than on the floor. It looked more comfortable. You don't mind, do you? I'm a very light sleeper, you see.' He blinked, golden eyes flashing.

'Oh. Er ... no, not at all,' mumbled Jack, climbing into the sleeping bag on the hard floor. He tried not to look surprised that Archie seemed to have put on Jack's best NASA pyjamas, without even asking. Or that he had clearly rearranged his precious fossil collection whilst Jack had been in the bathroom. 'That's no problem,' he said. 'You are the guest, after all. And it IS only for one night, isn't it?'

'Oh yes, just the one night. Goodnight, Jack.' Archie rolled over and turned off the bedside lamp.

'Goodnight, Archie.' But as Jack lay there in the darkness, staring at the ceiling, he began to feel a bit concerned. Not only was he behaving differently, if Jack wasn't very much mistaken, Archie Cuckoo had grown considerably taller since teatime.

8

Bamboozler

When Jack woke up the next morning, the bed next to him was empty. He looked at the alarm clock and to his horror realised he had overslept. Grabbing his uniform and scooting downstairs, Jack saw his mum sitting at the breakfast table reading the newspaper.

'Morning, Jack. Did you sleep well?'

'Hardly a wink. Have you seen Archie?'

She lowered the paper to reveal a big, beaming smile. 'Yes, he was up with the birds asking for cake. I stuffed him and stuffed him and *still* he managed to eat more. Such a lovely boy. He said I made the best cakes he had ever tasted.'

A silver moth perched on top of her head, opening and shutting its wings. Jack blinked in shock. He couldn't believe his eyes: *had Archie bamboozled his mum?* He had specifically asked him not to do that. Even Picklewitch, as naughty as she was, understood that rule.

'Mum,' he said clapping his hands right in front of her face, 'snap out of it. Aren't you going to be late for work? You're a doctor, won't there be sick people waiting to see you?' asked Jack.

'Oh Jack, don't worry,' she said, her eyes shiny and swimmy. 'Doctors take days off too, you know! Archie asked that I stay at home and bake chocolate brownies, so that's what I'm going to do. Hundreds and hundreds of them. He's a growing boy with SUCH an appetite.' She picked up a mixing bowl and wandered off looking for ingredients.

Jack frowned. Archie had taken his bed, his pyjamas and now he had bamboozled his mum. He'd gone too far.

Jack grabbed his school rucksack, opened the front door and marched out into the garden. 'Archie,' he shouted. 'ARCHIE! Where are you? Can I speak to you please?'

Archie was leaning against the trunk of Picklewitch's tree, arms folded, grin in place. His jacket sleeves seem to have shrunk and his trousers were now short enough to clearly show the top of his gold socks. Even the buttons on his waistcoat were straining. Had he grown even more overnight?

'Morning, Jack. Are you well?'

'No, Archie, I am not well,' said Jack, getting straight to the point. 'Did you bamboozle my mum?'

He chuckled. 'But of course, dear boy. I am a witch.'

Jack's fists clenched. 'Well I don't care if you're a witch, a watch or an itch, I told you to leave my mum out of it, all right?'

Picklewitch dropped out of the tree before Archie could reply, two boots landing with a resounding thud on the ground.

'Well, I for one am very glad he's doing some proper magic *at last*. I was getting worried there for a bit. Thought he'd gone soft.'

'PICKLEWITCH!' protested Jack. 'You're supposed to be on my side.'

Archie smiled at Picklewitch and unfolded his arms. 'Ah but, Jack, you can never really know the true nature of a witch. A witch can switch like the wind.'

Picklewitch whooped and punched the air. 'Now you're talking like a proper witch.'

'Well, I don't like it,' said Jack, feeling outnumbered. 'I like to know who my friends are.'

'Of course we're your friends, Jack,' cried Archie, eyeing Picklewitch. 'Really, I'm very sorry about bamboozling Ladymum. I was just having a bit of fun.'

'Yes, well,' Jack scowled. 'Just don't do it again, all right?' With it being just the two of them for so long, Jack was fiercely protective of his mum.

Archie had touched a nerve. 'That's my mum and she's off limits, get it?'

'Oh come on, Jack,' said Archie, putting his arm around his shoulders. 'I'm very sorry. Let's let bygones be bygones, eh? You know, I've just realised I never *did* show your teachers my special maps. Maybe I should stay just one more day . . .'

'Well,' said Jack reluctantly, feeling a little better since Archie's apology. 'It *is* Geography today and I know Dr Fourwinds would love to see them.' In truth this was the moment he'd been waiting for ever since Archie had arrived. Maps that once belonged to Darwin would be a school sensation. 'All right then. But you both have to be good. Promise?'

Picklewitch and Archie blinked their gold and green eyes, licked their fingers and crossed their hearts in unison. 'Promise.'

9

Skywest and Crooked

Geography lessons with Dr Emeline Fourwinds were never boring. The class didn't know which direction the lesson would take with her at the helm; they might begin in the Congo but end up in Sweden, via Prague and Trinidad. Sometimes they would start at the North Pole only to find themselves at the foot of Mount Kilimanjaro.

An elderly explorer, Emeline Fourwinds had circumnavigated the globe alone on five separate occasions, once equipped only with a swimming costume, a pet dachshund and a gramophone. She was, without doubt, one of the most interesting people Jack had ever met. As an added bonus, nothing seemed to shock her, so when Picklewitch shouted out random answers like TRAPEZE, PLUTO or LARD, Dr Fourwinds never failed to give her a gold star for effort and creativity. A bamboozle spell wasn't even necessary.

'So, children,' she began. 'I see we have a visitor in the class. Young man, please introduce yourself.'

Archie stood up and put out a gloved hand. 'Good morning, Dr Fourwinds. My name is Archie Cuckoo and, I, like you, have also explored the globe.'

'A fellow traveller,' she said, shaking his hand. 'How splendid.'

Picklewitch, who was as local as a nettle, yawned and gazed at the collection of chittering sparrows in the tree outside the window. Archie continued, undeterred.

'Yes, and today I have something to show everyone that I believe will amaze you.'

'Well well, do you indeed?' Dr Fourwinds lowered her half-moon spectacles, revealing crinkly, smiling eyes. 'I have seen many wonders in my long life young Master Cuckoo. I have seen eagles dance and mountains sing. I must warn you I am not easily impressed.'

Jack, bursting with excitement and unable to contain it any longer, put up his hand and waved it about. 'Honestly, Dr Fourwinds, Archie has something totally mind-blowing in his briefcase.' Jack reached out for Archie's case, only to have his hand smartly slapped by Archie's gloved one.

'Do not touch, please Jack,' snapped Archie, eyes frosty and smile brittle. 'I already have the item here in my desk.' Embarrassed, Jack's cheeks burned and his hand stung.

Archie lifted the lid of his desk and took out a scroll. 'As you will see, here is a map. It is dated October 1835. If you look at the top corner here you will see that it says HMS Beagle, Exploration of the Galapagos Archipelago, and down here you will see a signature.'

Keen to see what Archie had to show them, the whole class huddled around the desk. He rolled out an old, yellowing map. It featured small islands with names like Albemarle, Charles and Chatham, a meandering ink line weaving in and out of them. Little sketches of birds adorned the borders.

Dr Fourwinds eased her way through the crowd, adjusted her spectacles and inspected the map. As she did her eyes widened. 'But ... what ... Archie, where did you get this?' she demanded,

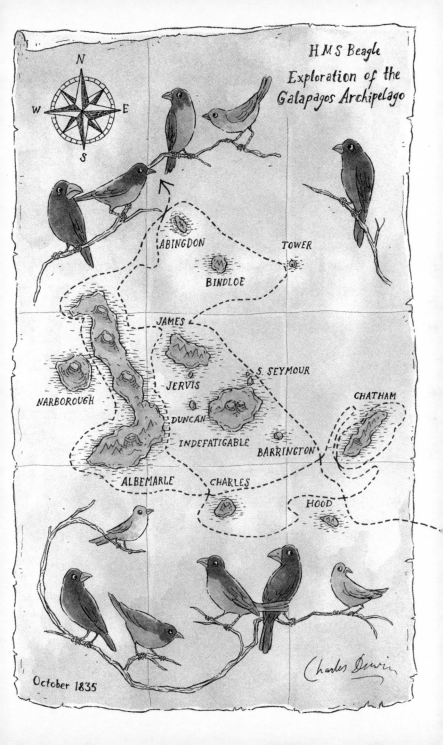

scrutinising the signature. 'This is signed by Charles Darwin.' Her fingers traced the lines of the sailing routes, of the sketches of creatures. 'Look,' she laughed, pointing at the map. 'Look at the illustrations of finches! Children, these are the studies that led to our understanding of evolution.'

She turned to Archie in amazement. 'If this is genuine, then it is priceless, not to mention incredibly important. Where on earth did you get it?'

'Oh you know,' said Archie, primping and preening himself in the window's reflection. 'One comes across interesting people on one's travels.'

Victoria elbowed her way to the front and threw her arm around him. 'I KNEW Archie was a special boy as soon as I met him,' she declared to the class. 'I knew straight away that here was a future star of St Immaculate's.'

'Well how kind of you to say, Victoria,' said Archie, grinning widely, accepting her offer of a blueberry muffin.

'I do hope this means we can be best friends, Archie,' whispered Victoria, fluttering her eyelashes.

'I can't think of anything nicer, Victoria,' said Archie, popping the cake in his mouth.

Jack looked around for Picklewitch for support but infuriatingly her chair was empty.

After scoffing Victoria's cake, Archie neatly dabbed away crumbs from the corner of his mouth with a monogrammed handkerchief. 'I also have something else to say. I would like to donate the Darwin map to St Immaculate's School for the Gifted.' There was a gasp, followed by a deafening round of applause.

'Goodness, Archie,' continued Dr Fourwinds, beaming. 'This is so generous of you. Headmistress

Silk will be over the moon. Not to mention Professor Bunsen. Oh my goodness, as a scientist he will hardly be able to contain his excitement . . .'

With a loud bang the classroom door swung open. 'THEY'RE GONE!' A wild-eyed Professor Bunsen stood in the doorway, raking his hand through his hair in panic.

'Septimus, are you quite all right?'

'NO I AM NOT! I AM NOT AT ALL ALL RIGHT!'

'What on earth has happened?'

'All my caterpillars, all 2,489 of them. THEY ARE ALL GONE! How am I supposed to conduct my research now?'

'My dear man,' said Dr Fourwinds soothingly, 'calm down. Creatures kept in a secure, atmospherically controlled room do not simply disappear. Why would they be missing? I'm sure

there is a perfectly reasonable explanation.'

'Well then,' said Professor Bunsen, sweating profusely, 'I would like to know what that is because they were kept under lock and key and no one but me knew the combination. It's impossible! It's like *witchcraft*!'

Archie stood up. 'Such terrible, dreadful news,' he said, rolling up the map and handing it to Dr Fourwinds. 'Professor Bunsen, we must find them quickly or it could compromise the experiment beyond repair.' He turned to the class. 'I was planning on leaving today but I couldn't consider abandoning the school in its hour of need. I shall stay just one more day to help with the search. My dear cousin and I will do our best to help, won't we, Picklewitch?' He looked round, eyebrows raised. 'Picklewitch? Oh my, how strange, oh where *can* she be?'

Victoria let out a long sigh, folded her arms and looked pointedly at Jack. 'Yes Jack, where IS she?'

10

Gobbler

That evening Jack lay in the sleeping bag on the floor, grinding his teeth and staring at the ceiling. Lying next to Archie, listening to his soft snores, Jack's bad feelings grew. Something was *very wrong*, but he couldn't quite put his finger on it. Archie might be smart and clever and polite, but there was definitely more to him than met the eye. Jack was secretly glad he was leaving tomorrow, even though they hadn't been able to find Professor Bunsen's creatures. Jack sincerely hoped that Picklewitch had had nothing to do with the disappearance but knowing how she felt about trapped animals – well, anything was possible.

Talking of Picklewitch, where had she gone? He wanted to talk to her about Archie. Her habit of suddenly disappearing was most inconvenient, especially as Archie had used up his welcome in the house. Jack tossed and turned, trying to get comfortable on the hard floor, his thoughts racing. Archie was supposed to be *her* cousin after all so really *she* should be taking care of him. Jack looked forward to everything getting back to normal, when it would be just him and Picklewitch again and everyone was in their own beds. Eventually, his thoughts began to slow down, his eyelids dip and drop, as he slipped into sleep.

Hours passed peacefully until, in the dead of night, he was jolted awake by strange noises.

Munch munch slurp snap chomp crunch

Jack froze, ears straining, trying to figure out what it could possibly be. Slowly he opened his eyes, just a tiny little bit, and peeped through his lashes. The scene he witnessed shocked him to the core.

Illuminated by the moon, Archie sat up in bed, the NASA pyjamas now stretched to bursting. On his lap was his open briefcase. He was taking fistfuls of something out, cramming them greedily into his mouth and gobbling them up. *Was it cake? Maybe biscuits?* However, as Jack's eyes became accustomed to the light he saw it was something much, much worse – *Professor Bunsen's caterpillars!*

Horrified, Jack shut his eyes tight and stayed as still

as he could, trying to get the vision of the green rubbery, hairy caterpillars out of his mind. The minutes passed like hours. Eventually Archie clicked his briefcase shut and lay back down to sleep. Jack waited and waited until he could hear soft snores and then silently wriggled out of his sleeping bag.

Jack was very good at remembering facts and the thing that had been niggling away at him finally bobbed up, cork-like in his memory. He crept over to the bookcase and slipped out his old tattered copy of *Birds of the World*. Trying to be as quiet as he possibly could, he clicked on his torch and flicked through the pages. He searched past *albatross*, *barn owl* and *chaffinch*. On page 48, halfway down, was the information he'd been looking for.

Cuckoo

Latin name: Cuculus Canorus

Arrival heralds the beginning of spring.

Appearance: Grey tailcoat feathers, horizontal
stripy chest, yellow eyes and feet.

Description: Solitary bird, arrives in the UK
having travelled from sub-Saharan Africa.
Grows at great speed, big appetite, eats
large amounts of caterpillars. Known as
a parasite bird because it lays its eggs in
the nests of other birds, disguising itself
as part of the family but with the ultimate
plan of ejecting all others.

Mimic. True masters of deception.

He looked at the illustration and then at Archie, duvet flung off and feet hanging over the end of the bed. That tailcoat and waistcoat looked grimly familiar, not to mention the yellow socks.

Jack clicked off the torch, shut the book and quietly placed it back onto the shelf, holding his breath, trying not to make a sound. He sat still for a moment, wondering if his heart sounded as loud outside his body as it did in his head. *What to do next?* But the answer was obvious.

Jack stood up, crossed the room and quietly opened the bedroom door out on to the landing. He tiptoed down the stairs, wincing at every creak, and stepped out into the cool stillness of the night to find the one person he knew would know what to do.

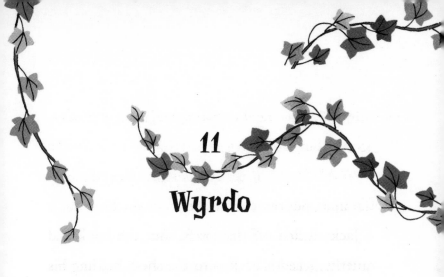

11

Wyrdo

Squeezing through the gap in the garden door, careful not to make it squeak on its hinges, Jack entered the garden. The moonlight made it nearly as bright as day and he could see everything quite clearly. He had been in such a rush he'd forgotten to put on a coat or even change out of his slippers. The leaves and twigs crunched softly underfoot as he crept through the undergrowth. 'PICKLEWITCH ...' he hissed. 'Are you awake? It's me, Jack.'

He could see her clearly in the moonlight,

sitting in her tree, wide awake and feeding crumbs to an upside-down bat.

'Picklewitch! Where have you been? Listen,' whispered Jack. 'I'm sorry to tell you this but I have something terrible to say about your cousin.'

'*What colour ...*' she pondered, appearing not have heard a word he'd said, 'is moonlight? Me and the bat-baby at are trying to figure it out. It's not exactly white or blue or grey or silver or pewter or pearl or milk. It's something else, it's like the thirteen o'clock of colours. That must be why it's so useful in spells.'

'Picklewitch! Did you hear what I said? I've got something important to tell you!'

She tickled the little bat behind his ear and made it squeak with delight. 'Oh all right. What is it then?'

Jack took a deep breath. 'I think Archie Cuckoo is a bad witch.'

She snorted. 'Is that all? Have you only just noticed? I knowed THAT as soon as he said he wanted to sleep indoors. Very peculiar. I mean, who *wouldn't* want to sleep in my tree? A fudgenut, that's who.'

'You knew?' asked Jack, feeling confused. 'But why didn't you say anything; he's your cousin after all!'

Picklewitch hummed and haa-ed. 'Well well. Maybe he is, maybe he isn't.' Picklewitch looked at the sky, at the tree, at the floor – anywhere but at Jack. 'In fact, now I come to think of it, I'm not even sure I have a cousin. Or any family at all for that matter.'

'WHAT?' Jack couldn't believe his ears. 'But . . . I thought you'd known him all your life! "Blood is thicker than custard" you said! It even said he was your cousin in the card!'

'Goodness me, Jack,' snapped Picklewitch. 'Who am I to question an official witch letter?' Jack put his hands on his hips and glared hard at Picklewitch until she held up her hands in surrender.

'Fine! All right! I've been rumbled.' She rolled her eyes and sighed. 'Look, I got carried away with the idea of having a cousin, all right? Is that so very bad? It's not my fault that the fudgenut made it all up. And, when you think about it, telling the truth is just a small thing.'

'Actually, no, I think the truth is quite a big thing,' said Jack.

'Littler than a bee's knee,' she continued, ignoring him. 'Tinier than a termite's toe. Anyway, while you were busy with boring old maps, me and the birds had a meeting. Turns out there's good news and bad news.'

'What's the good news?'

The good news is that because we is so clever we've unpuzzled it.'

'And the bad news?'

'Archie Cuckoo is a Wyrd.'

'A Wyrd? What's a Wyrd?'

'Well,' Picklewitch picked up her rucksack and began to rummage around inside it. 'There's all sorts of witches, just like there are all sorts of Boxies. Most witches know that sharing is important, but Archie isn't that sort of witch. He's more of a bad higgledy-jiggledy mix of stuff. You know, like kipper porridge or eggy cabbage.' She reached her arm inside until she was up to the shoulder, which seemed unusual to Jack as the bag was only the size of a beachball. Then, to his astonishment, Picklewitch climbed right inside the rucksack, pulled it up over her head and entirely disappeared! Her voice sounded far away, as if it was coming from a cellar. 'You see,' it echoed, 'Archie is both witch and bird. As I said, a Wyrd.'

The sound of boots clacking up steps got louder and louder until her head popped out of the top. 'Now, if he was part sparrow, say, then this would be all right, because a sparrow is a cheerful bird. Or a wren, cos they is funny as mustard. Even Kenneth the Kestrel can be reasoned with, unless you is simply *too* furry and delicious of course. But Archie is part cuckoo, which is very bad because they are short on sharing and big on fibbing. Selfish, tricksy birds they are, but it takes all sorts I suppose. All witches can't be as whizz-cracking as me, you know.' With considerable effort she clambered back out of the bag, grimoire in hand. 'I'd show you pictures but you know my Grim don't like Boxies.'

'Hang on a minute, where did you go just now?' said Jack, completely forgetting to whisper. 'I've looked in your rucksack and it has a bottom. Are you doing magic right now?'

'Bottoms?' Picklewitch looked genuinely perplexed. 'Magic? What a rude and personal question. Most certainly not. Are your books magic?'

'What do you mean?'

'If you open them up isn't there a whole world inside? Aren't they doorways to other places? Honestly, Jack, sometimes I think you are quite stupid.' She gave a big sigh. 'If you absolutely must know I am not *doing* magic, because the *bag* is magic all by itself.'

'Really? Wow! Where did you get it?' asked Jack, round-eyed with wonder.

'I won it fair and square in a fight with an owl. That's my story and I'm sticking to it. Anyway, that's enough questions for now. Please pay attention because this next bit is very serious.' She narrowed her ey. 'Archie Cuckoo is a nasty bit of work so we have to get rid of him. But if he thinks another witch has twigged him, the whole thing could turn ugly. So YOU are going to have to do it for me.' She took a dandelion clock out of her pocket and blew long and hard at him, the little seeds floating down and landing in his hair.

'ME?' Jack batted the seeds away. 'You must be joking – he's your problem not mine! Just a minute ago you said he was a bad higgledy-jiggledy witch and a nasty piece of work! A Wyrd? I'm just a human boy! Picklewitch, I don't even like going to the dentist!'

'Don't be such a fusspot Jack,' she said, turning back to the bat and smiling. 'Just make an excuse. I'm sure Archie will listen to you.' She gave a little smirk and popped a bug into the bat's open mouth. 'After all, you have *so* much in common, what with him being so *smart* and *clever* and *polite*. Just the sort of person you'd like to be friends with, I'm sure.' Jack blushed.

Picklewitch faked a big yawn and pulled her hat over her eyes. 'Anyway, I'm suddenly most terrible weary so cannot be talking to the likes of you. Bedward to the greenwood. Shut the garden gate on your way out.' And Jack knew that was the end of that.

As he trudged back through the garden, muddy puddle water seeping through his slippers and squidging between his toes, Jack had the distinct feeling that he had been out-played. Jack was rubbish at lying and their family motto was 'facts not fiction'. However, on this occasion he was just going to have to do it. He decided to pretend he was a writer, because they made things up all the time.

Jack crunched across the gravel back to the house. He was so busy sighing over his slippers and thinking about being a famous writer, he hadn't noticed the silhouette in the attic window – the figure that had been watching them the whole time.

12

All Things Bright and Beautiful

After a night of dreaming up increasingly unbelievable excuses, Jack awoke to discover that Archie had flown the nest of his own accord.

To his great relief the bed was completely empty. It had been made very neatly, NASA pyjamas folded at the foot. On the pillow was an envelope, addressed simply to 'Jack'.

He opened it and inside was a familiar notecard. In beautifully neat, ornate handwriting it said:

Dear Jack,

A gentleman never outstays his welcome. Thank you for your bed but now I must be on my way. Please say farewell to dear cousin Picklewitch for me and thank your mother for the delicious cakes.

Yours faithfully,

Archie Cuckoo

P.S. I took the liberty of cataloguing your fossils in chronological order, from the Palaeozoic to Cenozoic period. I hope this is all right.

So Archie Cuckoo had upped and left without Jack having to say anything! Jack felt an enormous sense of relief, quickly followed by a winkling feeling of self-doubt. Maybe Archie wasn't *that* bad. It was a perfectly polite and reasonable letter and his fossils did look very tidy indeed. Had they overreacted? Whatever the answer, it was too late now.

Jack got dressed, grabbed his rucksack and a piece of toast from the table and ran out of the door. 'Bye, Mum, I'm off to school.'

'Bye, Archie,' she called, her voice trailing away in the distance. 'See you later.'

By the time Jack got to the front gate Picklewitch was already waiting, carefully picking a family of snails out of her hair.

'Guess what?' said Jack, marching up the street, a spring in his step. 'He's gone!'

'*Gone?* Just like that?' she said suspiciously, sniffing at a snail. 'Hmm. Smells fishy to me. Witches is normally a lot more troublesome than that.'

'Yes, well Archie isn't like an ordinary witch, is

he? He's a Wyrd,' said Jack, with a definite hint of smugness. 'It's all right, you don't need to thank me. That's the end of the matter.'

Picklewitch sucked air through her tooth gap and looked sideways at the crow on her shoulder, who looked equally doubtful. 'With witches, things are rarely as simple as that,' she said.

'It'll be fine, stop worrying,' breezed Jack. 'Don't be a fusspot. Can we just get back to normal now? No more unexpected visitors for a while, eh?' He strode cheerfully along the pavement, whistling to himself. 'This is an excellent start to what I hope will be an excellent day.'

'Woss so excellent about it?' asked Picklewitch, kicking an empty can down the street.

'Well, it's assembly this morning and you love that. Then it will be the Head of House elections.' Jack turned and looked rather sheepish. 'I didn't say anything before, but last week I put my name down on the candidate list. Ever since we won the end of term quiz everyone's been really nice to me so I reckon I might even be in with a chance of winning.' Jack grinned, brimming with happiness and new-found confidence. 'You'll vote for me for me, won't you Picklewitch? Come on, I'll race you to school. On your marks, get set – GO!'

House assembly at St Immaculate's was held in the Grand Hall, an oak-panelled room with a high-vaulted ceiling and stained-glass windows the colour of boiled sweets. The floor was hard and wooden, however, and enough to turn the most patient child into a fidgety clockwatcher.

As contrary as ever, Picklewitch did indeed love assembly. It always put her in the best of moods, and she was even known to take her hat off so the person behind her could see.

This was because of two things; the first being the singing. Picklewitch adored a singsong, even though she was rarely in tune. Her favourites were the hymns about the countryside, about the hills and fields. She particularly liked 'All Creatures Great and Small', which she sang at the top of her lungs, occasionally pulling alarmed weasels out of her pockets and waving them about with great enthusiasm.

But even better than this was the rainbow of light that spilled over them from the tall stained-glass windows. Picklewitch was always astonished that nobody else could taste the colours: sweet, sharp orange, juicy cherry-red and crisp apple-green. While Headmistress Silk presented information on league tables and sponsored events, Picklewitch sat in the sea of children; eyes closed, tongue out – ready to catch the fruity, delicious flavours. She was so lost in bliss that she barely even noticed when Headmistress Silk asked: 'Before we move on to the vote for Head of House, would any student like to take the stage to tell us about interesting news or developments? Anyone?'

A hand went up in the audience. 'Yes! Me! Me!'

Victoria Steele stepped her way through the crowd and made her way up to the stage. There was a muted round of applause as she stood by the lectern and adjusted the microphone. Victoria was always making some bossy new announcement so no one was particularly surprised. But today she looked even more pleased with herself than usual. Jack felt suddenly nervous.

'Good morning everyone,' she trilled. 'I would like to take this opportunity to announce something very important, something that I have been trying to tell the staff here for a while. But as it seems no one will listen to me about it, I'd like to invite a very special friend to tell you instead.'

Picklewitch stopped licking at the light. On high alert, she snapped open one emerald eye and rolled it around the room. A whisper whooshed around the hall like a breeze in a field of wheat.

'I'd like to invite up on stage,' Victoria continued, 'Entomologist, benefactor and *my* personal best friend ... ARCHIE CUCKOO!'

13

Witchhunter

From behind the stage curtains stepped a familiar figure. 'What's HE doing here?' gasped Jack. 'He said he was leaving!'

Picklewitch muttered darkly, shaking her head. 'Told you not to get too comfy, didn't I? Witches *cheat*, as sure as eggs is eggs.'

Victoria stepped aside and ushered Archie to the lectern. Archie appeared to be bigger and taller than ever; his trouser legs only just skimming his shins, his sleeves ending halfway up his arms. His waistcoat buttons were under considerable strain, one even popping off and pinging across the hall and hitting the radiator. His nose was beginning to look suspiciously beak-like.

Archie cleared his throat and, as he did, a blizzard of tiny white feathers flew out of his gloved fist and settled on the audience like snow.

Picklewitch couldn't believe her eyes. 'Spadger's socks! Would you believe the nerve of the bird? That's MINE!' She whipped out her Grim and flicked through until she came to a torn page. 'Fudgefrazzlin' Wyrd's only gone an' stole my Boombazzle spell!'

'Boombazzle?' asked Jack. 'Don't you mean Bamboozle?'

Picklewitch was seething. 'No-no-no,' she snapped. 'Why would I mean that? Those words are completely different to each other! Instead of making everyone happy like a Bamboozle, it makes 'em proper angry. It's a curse – it's not safe!'

But the whys and wherefores didn't matter now, because everyone in the room – students and teachers and even Newton the cat – were all utterly transfixed by Archie. Hundreds of winged insects; butterflies, moths, dragonflies, bees and daddy-longlegs began to zoom around the hall as all good sense escaped out of their ears. Even the headmistress had a ladybird sitting on the end of her nose.

Picklewitch began to rage. 'It's a savage and dangerous bewitchin' all right. How DARE he? So much for the Witch's Code. Thievin' cheatin' rotten snollygaster ...'

'Dear friends,' began Archie, his golden eyes roaming around the room. 'Are you all listening carefully? Yes?'

'YES,' everyone chanted in unison, their spellbound eyes gazing up at him.

'I am here to reveal some terrible news ...'

'TERRIBLE,' everyone repeated.

'Right here in this room there is wickedness, disguised as your friend,' he said.

'WICKEDNESS.'

Jack looked at Picklewitch, a tide of fear rising in his chest. Picklewitch was silent, all but for the grinding of her teeth.

'Listen carefully to me dear friends,' continued

Archie, locking eyes with Picklewitch. 'I am sorry to tell you that the imposter, WHO IS IN THIS ROOM RIGHT NOW, is not a real human like you … and me, of course,' he added. 'Not only is she is a liar and a traitor …' He pointed directly at her hat and bellowed: 'I SAY SHE IS A TRUE WITCH!'

There was a gasp and everyone turned to look. Quietly at first, then louder and louder, the crowd began to chant: **'A TRUE WITCH!'** thumping their fists on the floor in time. Jack couldn't believe his ears. This was his nightmare – just like the scenes he had read about in his history books. How could this be happening here, of all places? Here at St Immaculate's School for the Gifted, where being different was supposed to be good?

Barely able to contain her glee, Victoria held up a scroll and unfurled it for everyone to see. Over

the chanting she cried, 'WE HAVE COMPILED
A LIST OF HER CRIMES:

1. She lives in a tree
2. She cheats
3. She is a liar
4. She talks to birds
5. She swears
6. She's weird
7. She smells of mushrooms
8. She makes Old Magic
9. She stole all of Professor Bunsen's caterpillars and ATE them!'

Jack could bear it no more. 'LIES!' he shouted, standing up and waving his fist. 'That's not fair! She doesn't ... she isn't ... well, she would NEVER eat those caterpillars!'

Picklewitch grabbed her rucksack and pulled the buckles tight. 'Time to go,' she muttered, shoving her way through the audience.

'Look!' cried Victoria, hopping up and down, hysterical with power. 'Look at the witch trying to escape!'

Archie pointed his finger: 'SEIZE HER!'

'SEIZE HER! SEIZE HER!'

Picklewitch broke into a brisk trot. She scrambled up the gym apparatus ropes and headed for the window. Two prefects snatched her by the boots as she tried to jump out.

'Gerroff me!' barked Picklewitch.

'Stop it! Leave her alone!' cried Jack, trying to pull them off her. 'Archie's the bad one, not her! Why won't anyone listen? Have you forgotten her jokes? The Nature Club? Picklewitch is our friend!'

But it was too late. In less than a minute Picklewitch's fortunes plunged from hero to zero and she was being dragged, kicking, to the headmistress's office: 'You've not heard the last of this, Archie Cuckoo, you mark my words,' she bellowed, 'you grubblin' fudge-frazzler!'

But Archie was deaf to her protests, chest more puffed out than ever. He raised a gloved hand to settle the raging crowd. 'Now then my little birds,' he smiled, looking down at the crowd gazing spellbound up at him. 'We reaches the part of the assembly where we cast our vote for the Head of House. Tell me Victoria, how many candidates is there?'

Victoria beamed. 'Just the one, Archie – you.'

'Me? Well, snapgrazzles and squarks, how perfect.' Archie's voice now sounded screechier, his accent and words changed. He stretched out his arms, threw his head back and launched into a song.

'From far away across the sea,
I flapped and swooped and flew,
To find a nest of my very own,
just for me (and not for you).
Bigger, taller, swell and grow,
Take my half and yours too.
I'm not the sort to wait my turn,
It's not what witches do.
The bubble's already 'round the room,
And my heart is filled with cheer.
Her magic it don't work no more,
'Coz I is master here.
So if you wants to vote for Archie,
all you has to do,
is sing loud and bright and clear:

CUCK-OO! CUCK-oo! CUCK-oo!'

They all erupted like a mad and terrifying cuckoo clock factory.

'CUCK-OO CUCK-OO
CUCK-OO CUCK-OO
CUCK-OO CUCK-OO
CUCK-OO CUCK-OO'

Jack knew a powerful spell when he saw one. He put his hands over his ears and ran for the exit.

14

Trapt

Jack hid in the bush beneath the headmistress's window, feeling scared and not knowing what to do. From here he could see Picklewitch stomping around the office, flinging her rucksack at the walls like a hammer thrower. While he couldn't hear the exact words she was saying, he knew they were very, very rude. He knocked quietly on the glass to get her attention.

Picklewitch span around. She marched over to the window and shouted more bad words.

Eventually, when she realised that Jack couldn't hear them, she picked up a notepad and began to furiously scribble away. She held the paper up to the glass.

Archie Kuk-coo
BAD BAD BAD FUDJNUT

'Yes I know that,' nodded Jack, 'he is!' She scribbled away again.

Carn't git owt
Majiks broke

'I know, he just did a big spell to stop it,' mouthed Jack. 'Don't worry Picklewitch, I'll help you!'

But how? The door was probably locked and, anyway, he could see the backs of the two prefects standing guard though the glass of the door. The office window was the only possible exit. He tucked his fingers beneath the frame and tugged for all he was worth, but it wouldn't shift.

Jack looked around and his eyes settled on a big rock. He hesitated for a moment. *Maybe he could smash it and Picklewitch could climb through?* Jack had never, ever smashed a window in his life, never mind one in a headteacher's office. He wondered if he would be arrested. But Jack was Picklewitch's only friend right now and he couldn't let her down. Jack picked the heavy rock, held it above his head and was about to hurl it through the window when Picklewitch slapped a page against the window:

	NO-NO
	roK not wurK!
	InesKape-a-bubbul

Jack put the rock down. *Inescapabubble?* Jack looked carefully through the window. A shimmering filmy rainbow of light curved around the edges of the room, covering the walls, floor and ceiling. 'Of course,' he thought, 'that's what he meant by *"the bubble's already around the room."'* That was why she had been flinging her bag around. It wasn't a tantrum – she had been trying to pop her way out!

Picklewitch slapped another scribbled page against the window:

	2 tuff for poppin.
	Trapt.
	Strong bad MajiK

She paused for a moment and then wrote on
another piece of paper.

> *Iz Veree bad*
> *Jak hlp Picklewitch.*
> *Kwik pliz thank yoo.*

Picklewitch pressed her hand to the glass,
fingerprints flat and grubby, her eyes full of alarm.
Jack didn't like this one little bit. Picklewitch
wasn't normally afraid of anything. He placed his
outstretched fingers over hers through the window
to let her know she wasn't alone, that they were in
it together. He tried to slow down his thoughts but
they came rushing in too fast. *What was Archie
planning to do with her? Would she be sent away?
What would become of the birds with no one to take
care of them? She had to get back to her tree and find*

her magic. He racked his brain trying to think of how she could escape. Jack was really good at riddles and puzzles but this one was too hard, even for him. *If the inescapabubble surrounded the room and her magic had been hobbled by Archie, then how could she get out?* Frustrated and desperate, Jack felt a lump stick in his throat and his eyes begin to prick with tears.

Then, just when it seemed that things couldn't possibly get any worse, Picklewitch suddenly froze.

'What's wrong?' said Jack, looking about urgently. 'What is it? Can you hear something?'

Picklewitch mouthed a single word: 'FOOTSTEPS.'

Like a ticket machine, Jack's very clever brain chose this moment to spit the answer out.

'Picklewitch, *your rucksack!*' He pointed at it in excitement. 'It's an emergency exit! You can use its

138

magic to escape! GET IN!'

Picklewitch's eyebrows shot up as she understood. Wasting no time she threw it onto the floor, unzipped the top, stepped in, gave Jack a gleeful wave – and dropped like a rock off a cliff. Instantly the rucksack folded in on itself once, twice, a hundred times and vanished into thin air.

Jack saw the handle on the door turn, but didn't wait around to see more. Holding in a loud cheer, he slipped out of the bush as quietly as he could and crept across the playground. He jumped over the wall, ran through the graveyard and raced for home. He didn't need to wonder where Picklewitch would be. Like all birds, she would fly home to roost.

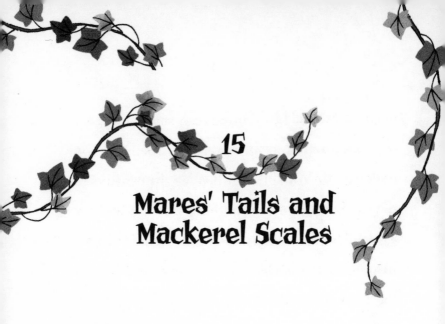

15

Mares' Tails and Mackerel Scales

The first thing Jack noticed as he reached the garden were the crows standing on guard. They lined the top of the wall, hunched and black, flapping in the wind like funeral bunting.

Jack squeezed through the gap in the garden door, wiping the cobwebs from his uniform, a strong smell of damp filling his nostrils. He looked about cautiously, trying to assess the mood of the garden.

The mood of a garden was not something that most people normally thought about, being far too busy looking at the flower beds or the ornaments to worry about this sort of thing. But the Rookery garden wasn't like that. Old and unruly, it had a habit of sharing its feelings as soon as you opened the gate. Sometimes it was warm and cheerful, tossing cherry blossom about as it basked lazily in the sunlight. Other times it fell into dark sulks, its pathways slippy with moss, shooting out sharp bramble whips from its borders to snatch and snag at passing ankles. It was rather like a wild creature, in that it didn't particularly trust strangers. Jack had also noticed that it often mirrored Picklewitch's state of mind. Today the mood was very black indeed.

He tiptoed through the undergrowth, trying not to upset the garden unnecessarily. *Where was she?*

He avoided the brambles and stepped over the nettles, skirted the mud and ducked beneath the spiny hawthorn. Finally he spotted her, arms around the trunk of her tree, rucksack slung aside.

'Picklewitch!' Jack cried with delight. 'You're home! Is your magic working again? Thank goodness! You must be so happy!'

But Picklewitch didn't turn around, her face buried in the trunk of her tree.

'What's wrong?' asked Jack, suddenly fearful. He noticed that the birds weren't singing.

Picklewitch let go of her tree and turned to look at him, her eyes red-rimmed. 'Just look at what that rotten Wyrd's done.' As she stepped aside, Jack saw the initials A. C. carved deeply into its bark.

Hundreds of birds sat on the ground watching, solemn as judges.

'Did he hurt you, poor tree?' she said. 'There, there, old thing, be brave.' She mashed up some nuts in a small dish and rubbed it into the wound. 'Don't worry,' she said, patting the tree gently, 'Picklewitch will make it all right.'

There was a long, heavy silence. Eventually Jack spoke. 'Picklewitch,' he said in a quiet voice. 'Will it really be all right? Because he seems like a really, really bad witch.'

Picklewitch didn't reply. She rummaged in the rucksack and pulled out her Grim, her expression changing from sorrow to thunder. 'Don't you fear. Picklewitch will make Archie Cuckoo pay,' she growled, snatching herbs from the undergrowth.

She laid the book on the ground and surrounded it with the plants. Then she reached into her pocket, took out a fistful of broken eggshells and sprinkled them on top. Finally she twanged out three hairs from her head and then reached over and plucked one of Jack's for good measure.

'Ouch! Is that absolutely necessary?'

Picklewitch narrowed her eyes and pointed her dirty fingernail at him.

'Are you's in or are you's out? This ain't school now, boy. I can't be dealing with mooncalves and frazzlers. This is real.'

Jack blushed. 'Yes yes, sorry. I'm in, of course I am. Sorry.' He plucked out another. 'Here, have another if you need it, I've got loads.'

Picklewitch looked up at him in astonishment, 'TWO Boxie hairs? Are you completely mad?'

'I ... I ... Sorry?'

'So you should be. Now, hush and shush and let me get on with my work.'

She carefully placed the strands of hair on top of

the eggshells and leaves and knelt down amongst the weeds.

Straightening her hat, she closed her eyes, wiggled her fingertips and began to clap her hands, slow at first, then faster:

'Grim, oh Grim
Oh Grim of mine
Rosemary, rue
Sage and thyme
Mares' tails and mackerel scales
Honey sun and gusty gales
Blackbird blue, lark and bee
Wise old Grim, find the key.'

Grim's pages flipped wildly back and forth, searching for the right answer. It flapped and fluttered like a winged thing until it finally settled on a page. Picklewitch leaned forward, read, smiled and nodded.

Jack wanted to see, so leaned forward too. But as soon as he did the book slammed shut with a bang.

'OI!' barked Picklewitch. 'I've told you before, my Grim is *private*. He don't like no one looking at him but me and *especially* not you.' She picked the book up and placed it back into her rucksack. 'I'll thank you kindly to remember that in future.'

Jack flushed pink. He remembered the last time he had looked at her Grim and had to admit that it hadn't ended well. 'Sorry,' he said again.

Picklewitch squinted up at the sky, then down at the sun's splintered reflection in a quivering puddle. 'No matter.' She dipped her finger in and examined it closely. 'I saw all I needed to see. Won't be long now,' she said.

'What won't be long?' asked Jack, looking

around. 'What do you mean? What's going to happen?'

'Archie Cuckoo is going to happen. He's on his way here right now, and if this puddle's to be trusted he's as angry as a sock full of bees.' She threw a walnut into her mouth, crunched it loudly and spat out the shell. 'But if it's a witch war he wants, then he's coming to the right address.'

16

Something Wicked This Way Comes

The sentry crows heralded his arrival, tearing the skies open with their cries.

'Right on time. You'd better get up in the tree, Jack,' said Picklewitch, straightening her hat in readiness. 'You'll be safer up there.'

Jack hauled himself up and managed to hide in a hollow between two branches just as the garden door creaked open.

'Picklewitch,' cooed an unmistakable voice, marching down the path. 'Oh *Picklewitch*! Is you in? Won't you be a-greetin' your dearest cousin Archie?' Instead of daisies and violets appearing in his footprints like last time, sharp thistles and Deadly Nightshade sprang up. Feathers poked out of every straining buttonhole and his yellow eyes were as hard as rivets. Finally, the **real** Archie Cuckoo had arrived in the garden.

Picklewitch stood in a little clearing, arms folded tight across her body. 'Felicitations and greetings, Wyrd. How are you this fine day?'

He tumbled into a slow cartwheel. 'I is well, tree-witch, thank you kindly for asking.'

Jack held his breath. *Why were they being so polite?*

The two witches bowed neatly to each other, stretching one leg out and then the other, like they were limbering up.

Ah, thought Jack. *This is like martial arts.*

'Beloved cousin of mine,' said Archie, cracking his knuckles and chuckling. 'Such a shame about the little misunderstanding this morning.' He pouted. 'Of course I didn't mean it.'

'Oh, dearheart, there's no misunderstanding.' She smiled sweetly and blinked her emerald eyes. '*I* thinks you know you is not *really* my cousin. *I* thinks you meant to get rid of ol' Picklewitch, to stealz her tree, her Boxie boy, the school *and* Ladymum all for your fat, greedy cuckoo self.'

Archie smirked and winked. 'It was just mischiffery dear one. Witches cheat, you know.'

Picklewitch continued. 'Cheating is fair. But you stand accused of something much worse – wounding a witch's heart tree. As every witch knows this is against the Code and is most deadliest of bad – deadly, deadly megabad. There is a price, and you, Archie Cuckoo, must pay.'

'Oh, *that*.' He didn't look even a little bit sorry. 'I have to say, well done on wriggling out of the Inescapabubble, what a tricksy little fish you are! You must have come up with something proper cleverish, eh?' He looked her up and down. 'And there was me thinking you was just a filthy stupid, little grubbler.' He held out a gloved hand. 'Is it time to dance, my dear?'

Picklewitch smiled. 'I thought you'd never ask.' She took his pristine glove in her muddy hand and they revolved around, slow at first, then faster and faster until their feet lifted from the ground. They whizzed and span, a vortex of dust whirling beneath them. They began to chant in unison:

ONE TWO THREE FOUR
TIME TO START A
WITCHING WAR,

TWELVETY-EIGHT, NINE AND FIVE SEE WHICH WITCH GETS OUT ALIVE!'

With a loud clap of thunder they burst apart and landed as smartly as cats, ready to pounce.

And they were off! Picklewitch was first out of the starting gate with a transformation spell. She hurled a fistful of nuts at him and cried 'TWANGLEFOOT!'

Archie looked down at his feet and gave a dry laugh. 'Is that the best you can do? Potatoes for feet? Oh dear.' He clicked his heels and they immediately returned to normal. He took a bright white shell out of his waistcoat pocket and crushed it in his fist. He blew the dust in Picklewitch's face, making her cough.

'Cherry red,
Sparrow's bed,
Ice stab at
That dirty head.'

A single black cloud appeared above Picklewitch and rained down big hailstones on her. 'OW! OW! OW!' 'There was a kerfuffle as all the sparrows panicked and burst out of her hair at once. Archie laughed and laughed.

'I'll wipe the smile off that beak, you just see if I don't.' She clicked her fingers in an odd, offbeat rhythm.

'Cockle buckle
Rattle pickle
Kettle spout
Secret's out.'

There was a flash and Archie's gloves and jacket sleeves disintegrated, revealing a pair of silken grey wings.

So that's why he always wore gloves – even in bed, thought Jack. *He's got feathers for fingers!* He gasped out loud.

'Jack?' Archie stopped what he was doing and looked up sharply. He cocked his head from side to side. 'Jack? Is that you, Jack? My dearest friend? Are you up there?' Jack froze.

'YOU leave Jack out of it!' shouted Picklewitch, fists clenched. 'You've never been a true friend in your whole long life. Even a *cat* would think twice about being friends with you!'

Archie sneered. 'Oh Picklewitch, don't be such

a grizzler. Look, let us stop this fighting and do a deal. Let me make it plain: I wants that Boxie boy and I've got something to swap for him.

'Swap? What you babblin' about, you dumbfoozle? Swap what?'

Archie called over his shoulder: 'YOU CAN COME IN NOW.'

The garden gate creaked. A girl's voice rang out over the garden: 'URGH! ARGH! Cobwebs! How horrible. What IS this awful place?'

Jack couldn't believe his ears. *Victoria?*

Victoria appeared around the corner wearing a glazed expression, an angry wasp buzzing around her head. Clearly bewitched, she picked her way through the weeds, pushing a large wheeled birdcage along. It was full to the brim with skylarks, nightingales, thrushes, blackbirds, wrens and robins.

'Thank you, Victoria. Just leave it over there,' instructed Archie. 'That'll do. I won't be needing your services any longer.' He gave her plaits a sharp tug and she slumped against the tree trunk in a deep sleep.

Picklewitch ran up to the cage and pressed her face between the bars. 'My poor little songbirds!' The birds looked up at her in miserable silence.

'Now,' said Archie, 'I'm prepared to return all of these birds to your garden in exchange for the Boxie boy and his cakey mum. Otherwise, I think maybe ...' he pondered for a moment and sighed, 'I will keep them trapped until they die of sadness.' He thought for another moment and nodded to himself. 'Yes, that is what I will do.'

Picklewitch shook her head in sorrow. 'First the tree and now this. You have turned on your own kind. Archie Cuckoo: you is the baddest and cruellest and wickedest witch there ever was.'

Archie laughed. 'Oh goodness, do stop, you're making me blush. Thank you kindly. Enough flattery. Now, do we have a deal or not?'

Up in the tree Jack sat stock still in anticipation, excited to see what mighty punishment Picklewitch would dish up to Archie for his unforgivable acts. One thing was for sure; it would be big and bad and amazing. 'Here it comes,' thought Jack with a smile, 'Any minute now ...'

Picklewitch gave a big sigh. 'All right Archie. You win. You can have 'em. Whatever you want, just set my songbirds free.'

17

Bad Stuff

What? *WHAT did she say?* Jack stopped breathing for a moment. *Had she agreed to swap him? Just like that?*

Before he could stop himself, Jack leapt to his feet and blurted out: 'NO! You can't swap me, Picklewitch! I'm not a sticker or a marble!'

Picklewitch looked away and shuffled her boots. 'Sorry, Jack, but I can't let the birds down. I'm afraid you'll just have to go with Archie. He's won fair and square. It's the rules.'

'But, but ... no! That can't be right – you're

supposed to be my best friend! You have to stick up for me! Like I stuck up for you just now, back there at school!'

Picklewitch shrugged. She looked smaller somehow. 'What can I say? Witches cheat. Sorry. No hard feelings.'

'Come now, Jack,' coaxed Archie, 'don't upset yourself. Down you come. All this magic has made me hungry. Let's go inside and see what our Ladymum's baked for our tea.'

OUR ladymum? OUR tea? What was he talking about? He suddenly remembered his mum's parting words that morning: Bye, Archie. Of course – she was still bamboozled! With this realisation, Jack's fear transformed into a boiling rage. 'Listen to me, Archie Cuckoo, she's MY mum and she'll never, ever be yours,' he shouted. 'And I'm not yours either! You'd better stay away from us or else!' Jack turned to Picklewitch. 'And as for YOU!' He picked up a walnut and hurled it at her in frustration, tears pricking his eyes. 'How can you betray me like this? This is what you get for trusting a witch. You are a total FRAZZLING FUDGENUT and I NEVER want to see you EVER again.'

Picklewitch looked crushed, her spirit broken.

'Jack,' warned Archie, 'I will not tell you again. I have been very patient with you. Come down from that tree right now or ... Oh!'

Archie peered down at the floor. Then he got on his knees and looked even closer. 'Are they ...' he sniffed, *cake crumbs?* Yes! Pink and yellow and chocolate cake crumbs! Yum yum,' he said, pecking away at them, crawling along on his knees. 'Yum

yum yum, these are the most delicious crumbs I have ever eaten. I can taste raspberry slices … and lemon iced buns … chocolate brownies and jam tarts … how absolutely scrumptious. It's like a rainbow of flavours!' Archie pecked and pecked, following the neat trail of crumbs up and down and through the garden on his knees. He seemed to have completely forgotten that Jack and Picklewitch were still there, so lost was he in his enjoyment of the tiny morsels. Winding back and forth, the trail eventually disappeared into a large, dark bush in the corner of the garden. 'I hope there is a big delicious cake in here,' murmured Archie. Unable to resist the lure of the delectable crumbs, Archie parted the branches of the bush and disappeared inside, the leaves closing behind him.

Picklewitch stood bolt upright; bright, sharp and grinning like a tiger. She held up her fingers and began a countdown: 'Five, four, three, two, one . . .' A mighty ROAR and SHRIEK shook the whole garden. Picklewitch looked up at Jack and gave him a big wink. 'BINGO.'

Blossom dropped from the trees and frogs hopped out of the puddles, panes shattered in the old greenhouse and the stone peacocks fell into the pond.

Of course! Jack clapped his hands together in delight. The bush labelled BEWARE on the garden map! What was it she had said? 'I would tell you what lives inside it, but I'm not the sort to give a guest the terrors on the first day.' Jack punched the air in victory – good old Picklewitch! How could he ever have doubted her? Picklewitch would never surrender to anyone. Who'd have thought that her talent for magicking crumbs would come in so useful after all?

After some more screaming, Archie eventually staggered out of the bush still clutching his briefcase, his feathers ruffled and his suit torn. The shock of the attack had made him cuckoo uncontrollably, like he had hiccups.

'You laid a trap, you rotten *CUCKOO* mugswoggling filth maggot,' spat Archie, 'but if you think that's going to *CUCKOO* finish me off you are even more stupid than you look. A powerful Wyrd like me isn't *CUCKOO* scared of a little grubbity witch like you!'

In his battered state Archie stumbled around the garden, falling into the Spiky bits, the Stabby bits and not forgetting the extremely icky, Squishy bits. Picklewitch put two fingers in her mouth and let out a piercing whistle. A kestrel swooped out of nowhere, snatching Archie's briefcase and hauling it high up into the clouds, flapping hard. Archie roared in anger as it became nothing more than a little dot. 'Come back! THAT'S MINE!'

Picklewitch cupped her hands and hollered, '*Now* please, Kenneth, thank you!' On command the kestrel dropped his cargo. The sky crackled

and darkened as the briefcase plunged to earth.
Picklewitch began to chant:

> 'Lightning spirits
> I call on thee
> Set the little wrigglers free.'

A bolt of lightning shot through the clouds and
struck the briefcase, illuminating the sky with a
white flash. The case exploded like a lepidopterist's
firework, releasing thousands of caterpillars into
the clouds.

'MY DINNER,' wailed Archie, as they rained down, '*CUCKOO-CUCKOO!*'

Now blind with fury, Archie made a wild grab for Picklewitch, but she was ready for him and neatly stepped aside. Missing his target, Archie fell headfirst into a big pile of leaves next to the potting shed. He lay there momentarily, cursing and spitting, getting his breath back.

Finally Archie hauled himself up, only to become aware that the leaves beneath him were humming. At first it was a buzzing, then a definite growling. Then, vibrating violently, they began to rise up and form a spiral around him. Rushing together, they climbed and climbed until they formed a single, giant silhouette.

Picklewitch squealed happily and did a little dance on the spot. 'Oh well done, Archie! Hooray hooray! You've woken up the Stormbeast!'

To Jack's disbelief the wolfish shape grew larger and darker, darker and larger. It rumbled and loomed over Archie's cowered form, baring its teeth and snarling as if to say *how DARE you come into our garden? How DARE you threaten our Picklewitch? I shall eat you in one snappilicious bite.* Archie shrank beneath the Stormbeast, covering his face with his wings and quaking. 'No! Stop! All right all right, I give up,' he whimpered. 'You win, just let me go!'

Picklewitch stood, hands on hips, birds cackling wildly in her hair, booming with laughter. 'Really?' she said. 'Oh dear, how sad. And I was having so much fun! But I am the best of hosts and, if you insist, then your wish is my command, Archie Cuckoo.' She clicked her fingers and the Stormbeast obediently transformed into a tornado, sweeping Archie into its heart and rising

up, up up, whirling him over the wall.

'Fly away, fly away and don't come back another day!' she sang as the Stormbeast carried him over the streets and houses, over the fields and over the sea, never to return to the Rookery garden ever *ever* again.

'Well,' she said, dusting off her dungarees. 'That certainly learned HIM a thing or five. Now . . .' she said, looking up at Jack, 'down to the important stuff. What's for lunch?'

18

Boombazzlectomy

It took a while to sort everything out, not least because the school was swarming with every kind of winged insect imaginable. Picklewitch had to work very hard all afternoon reversing Archie's Boombazzle one person at a time, reuniting them with their own personal insect. Even Professor Bunsen had been bewitched by this time, such was its power. His creature was an Elephant Hawk-moth and very difficult to squash back into his ear.

While she worked, Picklewitch explained that

she had accidently won the Boombazzle in a witch raffle, years before. Being a 'bad and wonky' spell she knew it would be dangerous in the wrong hands, so had kept it in her Grim for safe-keeping. She hadn't thought that Archie would take it when she wasn't looking. They both agreed he was a terrible fudgenut.

Eventually everyone was almost back to normal, although they were very confused by the feathers on the floor and the scroll on the stage. What did it mean? Who was it supposed to be about? Was it a poem? If it was meant to be a hymn then it was very strange indeed.

It had taken Jack and Picklewitch a while to walk Victoria all the way to school too as she kept sitting down and making cuckoo sounds. When they got her back, Picklewitch rubbed leaves on her cheeks and gave her scoops of honey from walnut shells but she still sat in the chair as stiff as a shop dummy, long after everyone else had come around.

'She got too close to him, see,' said Picklewitch, fiddling with Victoria's ear. 'It's very tricky getting her wasp back in. This one is so very, very cross.'

Jack had a sudden thought. 'Hang on a minute,' he said, 'if it's such a powerful spell I don't understand why I wasn't Boombazzled like everyone else.'

Picklewitch plugged Victoria's ear shut with a small cork and sighed. 'Do you remember the night you came out to the tree to tell me Archie was a bad witch?'

'Yes, you were feeding a baby bat.'

'Yes, well, I put an umbrella spell on you, just in case.'

'An umbrella spell?'

'On your head. It's a spell that keeps you safe from harm. You just think they're dandelion clock seeds but that's because Boxies don't know nothing.' She turned back to Victoria. 'Come on now Victoria, wakey-wakey or I'll have to give you a good shake!'

Jack thought for a minute. Then he felt around in his hair and picked out a tiny little seed, a fluffy little umbrella. 'So you did,' he marvelled, 'in the moonlight! I had no idea that's what you were doing.' He put the dandelion seed in his blazer pocket for safe-keeping. 'So does that mean that Archie could never have won anyway? Does it mean that you knew I would be safe all the time?'

'What can I say Jack?' said Picklewitch with a wink. 'Witches cheat.'

Suddenly Victoria sat up straight and looked around in surprise. 'What am I doing here?

What's going on?' She looked in disgust at Picklewitch. 'Ugh, dirty girl! Why is she touching me? Why am I covered in cobwebs? The last thing I remember I was up on the stage about to tell everyone about . . .'

'Your latest recipe!' cried Jack, suddenly discovering that telling a white lie wasn't as hard as he'd thought. 'Cherrydrop cupcakes. They really were amazing. In fact we ate them all. Everyone was very impressed. Don't you remember? We all . . . er . . . sang songs about weasels and then someone said we were going to have the vote for Head of House.'

Overhearing this, Headmistress Silk stood up, her hair rather messier than usual. 'Yes! That was it!' she said, tottering towards the stage. 'It's time for the Head of House Election.' She looked around at the disarray in the hall. In a stern voice she said, 'Goodness gracious. This is St Immaculate's School for the Gifted so kindly sit down on your bottoms, sit up straight and pay attention.' She clapped her hands. 'Quickly quickly. It's time to get on with the business of the day.'

19

Just Desserts

Dear Journal,

Everything's been so busy lately I forgot to write anything in in here! Lots of good things have happened since Archie left. Here is a list:

- *Professor Bunsen has forgotten all about his caterpillars because he's doing research into the freak tornado that was spotted near the school instead. The newspapers reported on it and everything. He's planning a new book called* Weather Wonders.

- *Dr Fourwinds took the Darwin map on the train to the Natural History Museum in*

London. The experts there got very excited and paid her lots of money for it. Picklewitch had a 'chat' with her and now the money's to be spent on new stained glass for the Great Hall. It's to be called The Window of Weasels.

+ The lunchtime Nature Club is more popular than ever, especially since Picklewitch taught spiders to cartwheel down people's arms and back up again. Everybody loves that, except for Victoria of course. Talking of her, she still looks at Picklewitch suspiciously but I don't think she remembers why. The funny thing is, every time the cuckoo pops out of the clock in the school office she jumps a mile high!

+ After Archie's briefcase exploded, the caterpillars must have fallen in amongst the weeds because now it's full of hundreds and

*thousands of moths and butterflies! They
are pollinating the plants so the garden is in
a permanently good mood. But even better,
at night they all light up like little lamps!
Picklewitch says it's the lightning strike that
did it. One is perched on my journal and
lighting up my page right now.*

* *Oh yes and one more brilliant thing – I was
voted Head of House!*

On the day Headmistress Silk presented Jack with his Head of House badge, his mum prepared a special celebration tea. Jack was so thrilled at the news he went straight out into the garden and invited Picklewitch inside to be his special guest. There was just one condition: NO bamboozling. Smelling the delicious wafts coming from the house, Picklewitch readily agreed.

They both sat at the table, Jack with his new badge on his blazer and Picklewitch managing to keep the birds firmly under her hat. The table had been set out perfectly, with china teacups, a teapot, napkins and silver cutlery. Picklewitch was determined to prove she could behave, only wiping her nose on the tablecloth once.

Jack cleared his throat. 'Picklewitch, I want to say I'm really sorry for not seeing Archie for the bad witch he was,' said Jack, looking awkward.

'Sometimes the way a person looks can give the wrong idea of who they are.'

'S'all right,' said Picklewitch, fiddling with her cake fork. 'You're only a silly Boxie, after all. Nobody's perfect.' She caught sight of her reflection in the mirror and added, 'Well, nearly nobody anyway.'

Jack picked up a plate and offered her a big, sugary jam doughnut.

'Thanking you most kindly I'm sure,' she said, stuffing the whole thing into her mouth in one go, gulping it down like a pelican. She let out a loud burp, her eyes popping. 'Oh dear,' she said primly, 'pudding me.'

Jack tried not to laugh. 'You mean pardon me.'

'Noes, I don't.'

'Yes, you do.'

'NOES, I DON'T.'

Jack eyed her closely. He couldn't help noticing

that steam was coming out of her pockets. 'Picklewitch,' he said suspiciously, 'are you about to do something naughty?'

'Certainly not and how dares you suggest such a thing,' she said, gritting her teeth and squeezing her eyes shut in concentration. 'Picklewitch don't need no Bamboozle spell to look good. She is the bestest at being good.'

'Well I'm pleased to hear that,' said Jack, keeping an eye out, 'because my mum will be back any minute.'

Picklewitch fidgeted in her chair, crossing her legs, folding and unfolding her arms. She puffed and panted, her face going red with the effort of trying to stay still. She threw a handful of sugar cubes in the air and completely missed her mouth. Then she picked up the teapot and drank from the spout.

Jack frowned. '*Manners*, Picklewitch.'

But Picklewitch's naughtiness was like a sneeze that could only be held in so long. With a whizz, pop and a bang, she shot out of her chair like a rocket. 'WHEEEE!' she squealed, landing boots-first on the table, sending the teacups clattering. 'Down with fandanglery and trumpery!' she crowed, kicking the napkins and teaspoons flying. With a twinkle in her eyes and a giggle in her guts, she whipped off her hat, sending a celebration of sparrows into the air.

'*NOBODY*
tells ME what to do BECUZ …
I DUZ what I LIKES
and I LIKES what I DUZ
OH YES!'

THE END . . .

NATURE KLUB
MEMBERSHIP ROOLZ

* Must Kno the secret password
P**K**W*T*H (Kloo: best
friend ever).
* Must Kno 5 different treez and
that walnut is top.
* Must wear Klub badge 2 meetings.
Leafs or shells is gud (beetlez,
snaylz and spyderz better).
* Must sware on Klub oath:
'I promise to do my best to be
gud to Nature OR ELSE.'

WEATHER PHENOMENON ON CORVID STREET

Yesterday, just before lunch, a powerful whirlwind mysteriously appeared near a house called Rookery Heights. Bystanders report seeing a tornado of leaves rise out of its garden, up into the clouds and then head south. Other witnesses spoke of the air being full of grey feathers and weird bird noises. 'It sounds peculiar I know,' said one elderly resident, 'but the tornado looked just like a wolf. My dear old cat Fluffchops was so scared he spat out his milk.'

Professor Septimus Bunsen, research scientist and teacher at St Immaculate's School for the Gifted, has confirmed that it was most likely a result of the unusually warm weather conditions for spring and that there is nothing to be alarmed about. He has been awarded a grant to look into it.

OWL FIGHTING ROOLZ

* Staring = gud

* Head swivelling = gud

* Bad langwidge = bad
  (TWIT speshly)

* Tikkling = bad

* Most interesting coffed up
  thing wins

CRUM SPELL

Britey litening, acorn drums

Robin's hikkup

Here it comes

By the pricking of my thums

In my hands be

MAGIC CRUMS!

DANCEY ANT SPELL

Tinee little beasteez

Tap dancing in the treez

Tinee little toez and

tinee little kneez

twirl and jump in tyme

dancing is a breez

Picklewitch would be grateful

Thank-you-veree-much-pleez

GLOSSARY

New Wurds

Boxie – person who lives in a house. Who knows why?

Wyrd – half person/ half burd.

Pebble – not a peacock

Proper dandy – beautiful (Picklewitch)

Yumcious galumpher – big delishus cake

Heart tree – See Yggdrasil. Magic. Secret. Shh.

Moonpuff – coff

Mischiffery – nortiness

Dumbfoozle – fudgenut

Cat – pongs of fudgenuttery

Lickspittle – fudgenut

Snollygaster – fudgenut

Grubblin' fudge-frazzler – Archie Cuckoo

PICKLEWITCH TOP 5 HAIRSTYLING TIPS

* NEVER WASH IT. EVER.
* Throw things at it. If they sticks, this is gud.
* Smell must be bad enough to friten skwirrulz.
* Once a year dip in puddlewater and shake like a wet wulf.
* Decorate with twigs and moss. Maybaps badger's teeth for parties. Shiny.

Warning: Do not let too many burds move in or you will topple over your boots.

WYRDIPEDIA

Wren wyrd – Funny as mustard

Blackbird wyrd – Smart
  as paint

Sparrow wyrd – Cheeky
  as chips

Chicken wyrd – Just weerd

UMBRELLA SPELL

Tick tock fluff, mount the air

Landing soft in your hair

Safe from harm and
  always well

Huff and puff umbrella spell

X-TRA STRONG
SPELL INGREDIENTS

Adder venom

Heart of dragon

Boxie hair (only ever use one or
BOOM!)

Toothpaste lids

HOW 2 SMELL NYCE

* Mash up mushrooms. Rub juice
under armpits. Repeat.

HOW TO RAISE A BAT

* Night burds must have their eyes
  polished every nite.
* Sing to them, but quietly (because
  of their big ears).
* Bedtime stories must be read upside
  down and backwards or they won't
  make any sense.
* Toast crums. Mayke them strong.

BOOMBAZZLECTOMY

Level: Middling

* Mix together bunny and
  cobwebs. Stikky.
* Add holly sprinkles.
* Dose: harf a walnut shell.
* Rub face with leaves.
* Push wing-beast back in earhole.
  Plug with cork.

CLAIRE BARKER

Picklewitch and Jack

A story about
two very
unlikely friends!

Illustrated by
Teemu
Juhani

Have you read Picklewitch and Jack's first adventure?

The dreadful strangers moved in on a wild and windy Thursday.

'Fudgenuts,' cursed Picklewitch, adjusting her cracked binoculars to get a better view of the comings-and-goings. 'This won't do at all. I bet they haven't even bought me any cake.'

Picklewitch lives in a tree at the bottom of the garden. She has a nose for naughtiness, a mind for mischief and a weakness for cake. And unluckily for brainbox Jack – winner of the 'Most Sensible Boy in School' for the third year running – she's about to choose him as her new best friend . . .

And look out for Picklewitch
and Jack's next adventure,
coming in Autumn 2020!